THE

MW01534499

CHRONICLES
VOLUME I

AM KRUSE

COPYRIGHT NOTICE

©A. M. Kruse

All rights reserved. No part of this publication may be reproduced, distributed, or transmitted in any form or by any means, including photocopying, recording, or other electronic or mechanical methods, with the prior written permission of the author/publisher, except in the case of brief quotations embodied in critical reviews and certain other noncommercial uses permitted by copyright law. The author/publisher is not responsible for websites (or other content) that are not owned by the author/publisher.

This book is a fictional work. Characters, names and events are the product of the author's imagination or are used fictitiously. Any resemblance to actual events, locales, or persons, living or dead, is coincidental.

Library of Congress Control Number: 2018906108

DEDICATION

For my momma, Betty Shively

No words could be put to pen to truly ever

express the depths of your love and

how it has shaped me into

the woman I am today.

I love you, too.

TABLE OF CONTENTS

PROLOGUE

I was born Beau MacClaflin, but who I was no longer matters. All who knew me are gone from this world. Any record that I existed has long since been erased; I am but a ghost. The front man for a team of three operatives, directed by a branch within the CIA and using the call sign Glaive, I worked hand-in-hand with two brothers - Mace and Axe. Together they referred to us as the Holy Trinity - we took the jobs that others failed.

We ate, worked, and lived together for three years. We had access to the agency through only one contact - our handler Huron. We knew from the beginning if something happened to him, they would come for us. "Forced retirement" they called it. If a handler is compromised, they "clean" the whole team rather than risk further exposure. We had never met Mr. Huron face-to-face, and now we never will. Apart from the initial files he was given Huron knew only what we allowed him to know about us. However, we knew everything about him. To survive in this game, you walk a fine line between hyper-vigilance and paranoia or you don't last long.

Shortly after we were given our last assignment, Huron failed to make a scheduled check-in. Sensing a trap, we took it slow, fairly certain it was an attempt to scrub our team. Mace disappeared while on recon. Axe and I went in to locate and retrieve him, but we hit heavy resistance during ingress. They dangled Mace's body from a window above us, causing Axe to break cover in his rage. I watched as a kill shot took down the last person I trusted. Enraged, I burnt that place down around me, barely making it out alive. I should have protected them but protection isn't exactly what I do. Still, I should have done more. I should have been better.

If the agency doesn't believe I'm dead, then they are hunting me now. I have no permanent home. I have no pattern for them to track. I siphon money off of those I take down as payment for services rendered, and I live off-grid. I leave no trail. If they can find me let them come, but I won't wait meekly to be slaughtered. My father didn't raise a quitter. No, I won't stop till I have avenged my team – my family. My name is Beau MacClaflin. Who I was may not matter, but who I am becoming is far more dangerous.

CHAPTER ●─────── ONE

I watched from the shadows as my target quietly made his way in to kiss his little girl goodnight. If I had been here for other reasons, I may have found the sight of him brushing her hair aside and kissing her cheek touching.

"Hello, Conrad." His body went stiff at the sound of my voice. He reached for the lamp that I had moved from her nightstand, knocking down the doll I put in its place. "I wouldn't do that. After all, if you see my face we both know what I will be forced to do." I clicked my tongue and whispered, "We wouldn't want little Emily to wake up and find you like that, now would we?"

He moved protectively in front of the sleeping child stammering, "Let's go downstairs and discuss this in my office."

A chuckle escaped me as I said, "No, I think you will be much more receptive with Emily near."

His voice trembled. "Glaive?"

Disgust dripped from my lips. "Conrad, you know better than anyone that the members of the Holy Trinity are dead. You gave the order. You sent us to die." I cocked my gun and he jumped at the sound.

"Let's think of me as their avenger. You will call me Bird, as you personally made me a bird of passage."

His voice cracked as he asked, "How did you get in here?"

"You don't know what you trained me to do, do you Conrad? You have become so fixated on results you have grown ignorant of how we get them – let alone the cost." I crossed the room, shoving his face against the door, ramming my gun into the base of his skull as I whispered, "Do you think so little of my skill set that you thought those two mall cops outside would be an issue for me?"

He struggled for breath. "What do you want?"

"You." I tossed him back into the center of the room and laughed quietly. "I have come for a new handler. You see, Conrad, I like my work."

"I'll get you someone...someone good," he pleaded, "and I'll scrub your old file...create a new identity so they won't know it's you. You want a new team, or to turn specialist? I'll make it happen," he pleaded.

"No, you misunderstand, Conrad." I smirked at his ignorance. "You aren't recruiting me." I let that sink in before I continued. "You're my asset now. You will act as my handler - one less likely to be compromised or canceled. In return, you can take credit for the all my hard work. In fact, want you to

2

use those victories to advance your career and gain access to the information I need. Together we will avenge my team."

The light from the window revealed his head shaking no. "I can't hide something like that and I wouldn't know how to track you."

I chuckled, "This is why I chose you Conrad, but I had no idea you would be so funny. You won't be tracking me, I'll be tracking you." I un-cocked my gun; he was no threat. "Downstairs in the bottom drawer of your desk you will find a package with instructions. Periodically a new one will arrive with additional instructions. You will follow them exactly as outlined. Nod your head if you understand me."

He nodded his head fervently in the moonlight. "I understand, but I can't stop them from hunting you, Glaive. They won't stop until you're dead, you know too much."

"Did I say you could talk?" I asked as I shoved a gun in his hand. "After tonight they won't." He pointed the gun at me pulled the trigger repeatedly, drawing a new chuckle. "Conrad, you're too predictable, and dare I say an ingrained coward. Glaive is downstairs in your office." I paused as he realized I had brought a dead body into his home. His shock forced a yet another smile to my lips. "Your back-up is on their way and will find you standing over her dead body, protecting your family." I pushed past him to the window. "I am counting on you getting a promotion for killing me."

I slid a leg out the window to the sound of several cars screeching to a halt in front of his drive. "Better get downstairs, hero." He started for the door. "Oh, and Conrad..." He stopped and turned toward me, hanging on my every word. "Don't make me come back here. I do so hate collateral damage." I motioned toward his sleeping daughter.

I heard his sharp intake of breath. "Glaive, you don't kill children."

"You killed the honorable Glaive. Who knows what Bird will do? She has nothing to lose. Ask yourself if it's a truth worth exploring. I *will* come for you and no one will ever find your body. Anyone that gets in my way will join you, innocent or not. Think about that the next time you contemplate betraying me." I jumped to a branch just outside the window and disappeared into the forest.

My plan was simple. Incapacitate my enemy by making him the hunted, and use him to feed my adrenaline addiction. Being watched has an inhibitory effect on cowards. Yet a sulking dog can be dangerous, and bears close watching to ensure it doesn't turn on its master. As such, I kept close watch on my new asset. It was hard to believe that men such as Conrad were making the decisions behind our wet work. He made himself such an easy target, same routines almost every day. I would be hard-pressed to keep him alive through a hit if I left him in his current environment. But Conrad is smart, ambitious and knows how to climb the promotion ladder; making him the perfect candidate to retrieve the files I need to avenge my team.

Over the next six months, Conrad and I got our feet wet with a few easy single-target ops without any hiccups. He approved of my silent, effective style. Not that I cared about his success rate, it was merely a means to an end, but a girl does like to be appreciated every once in a while. Our arrangement was proving mutually beneficial, and I found that being a single-person team was rather liberating. It allowed more freedom for my affinity for covert warfare, something that Axe had no patience for as he was more of a "if it moves, shoot it" kind of a guy. Still, I have to admit knowing someone you trust is there to cover your back was a hard thing to lose.

I pulled out my laptop, ran through my security check while dialing in for my next assignment. My laptop demanded, "Enter security code now."

"Bird–Tango-1– 9er," I replied.

After a sequence of beeps the laptop replied, "Hello, Bird, waiting for second party verification, please hold."

Conrad connected, "Watcher–Delta–725."

Satisfied, the computer acknowledged, "I have Watcher; your line is secure for the next forty-two seconds."

Conrad went straight to the point. "We have a delicate melodrama we would like you to review."

I inquired further. "A mystery?" Conrad's need for code was amusing but I played the part. I knew my end was secure but Conrad may have cause for concern and I was too close to my goal to lose him now.

"Yes, something I believe you would enjoy. Its villain is quite inhumane, and if left unchecked would unsettle our modern society at the very least. I am sending you the script now for your approval."

"Subtitles?"

"Not this time, this is an American film. Let me know when you're done editing or if you're declining the job." Conrad sent the file and disconnected.

I swept the incoming file for tracing programs before opening it. I was rarely approached for domestic ops, preferring to use my foreign contacts for munitions. My assignment was to weaken a textile company in Texas. This was a two-target job.

They wanted one target eliminated while the other could be left severely weakened, it was my choice as long as room was made for the operative they had in place to be promoted. My job was made more difficult as the previous team had botched the first attempt and put the targets on alert. A car accident? Are you kidding? They must be fresh from the farm, completely lacking in imagination - an easy way to be short-lived in this business.

Intel showed their company was a front for human trafficking. I would confirm that with my own recon; Conrad's intelligence team was a joke. Simply more people hiding behind the curtain, content with their role in the game, lying to themselves about how important they were, and often making assumptions with no basis in fact.

The following week was even less exciting. I never missed Mace more than when I was forced to do his job, but gathering information about your intended target was a necessary evil. Humans weren't the only product they were moving. One item in particular would be getting some added attention from me as soon as I completed this mission. If I lifted one of their weapon shipments, I would be able to stash a fair-sized load for a rainy day – always a nice surprise, and too good an opportunity to pass up.

I watched each of them for days, noting their

routines and those of their security team. When they slept, I pored through my notes planning carefully down to the exact time of each attack. It took an additional week of prep to procure my weapons of choice, but I was satisfied that my methods would prove lethal and be dramatic enough to impress Conrad's superiors. One last promotion for him should get me the information I needed regarding Trinity's final mission. I may not have been able to avenge my father when he died, but I was going to avenge Axe and Mace.

One last detail and I was ready to end this assignment. I went to the post office and bought a Houston postcard and a stamp. I quickly wrote a note to Conrad to inform him I was taking the job in his requested archaic spy-craft methods.

Aunt Zoe,

>*Yes I am in Houston and having a wonderful time. My bus leaves on Tuesday, so please have my things ready. I heard your favorite show earned another award, time to pay up on our bet.*

>*Love always, your little bird.*

I smirked to myself as I reread my message then tossed the post card in the outgoing mail.

Cutting the head off a snake is always a good idea, so I decided that the senior partner would be the one to die. His biggest weakness was his desire for younger women. Imagine that, how original. The world will be better with one less man that thinks with his dick. Yes, I like that...Death by dick! It would serve him right for cheating on his wife. Posing as a high-end call girl, though distasteful, would prove easy enough; from there I would use his peanut allergy as the final nail for his coffin.

Dealing with his junior partner would take a bit more finesse to ensure no one suspected my tampering, but I was looking forward to the challenge. I decided to use his asthma to take him out of play, leaving his life to fate. Well, fate and the skill of the doctors treating him. It had taken almost a week for the lab assistant to deliver the MRSA pneumonia specimen I had asked for, but the highly infectious nature coupled with the rarity made it the perfect weapon for this assignment.

Timing and preparation would be the keys to success, but I was confident my plans would work and be ruled accidental. Tonight, the senior partner had a date, and I was ready to make my move.

I waited in the shadows till the junior partner and his family sat down for dinner, then slid down the hallway to his bedroom. A quick search revealed the small canvas bag I saw him take each day on his run in the park. I pulled the contents out, laying them in order on the bed so I could repack the bag exactly, leaving no trace of my meddling. After locating his asthma inhalator; I took the canister out, doctored it with the MRSA specimen, and put it back in the actuator ensuring the counter displayed the correct amount of remaining puffs. As soon as my weapon was in place I restocked the bag and quietly moved to my next target across town.

Once there I waited in the lobby pretending to be on the phone till I spotted my prey, a young blonde making her way across the foyer. I hung up the phone barely beating her to the elevators. I smiled, openly appreciating her beauty and was rewarded. "After you," she offered while motioning to the empty elevator.

"Thank you." I moved past her to the back corner positioning myself under the camera careful not to provide a full shot of my face. The call girl moved to the panel and hit the button for the ninth floor. She looked over her shoulder at me with a questioning glance.

"Eight, please." I smiled as sweetly as possible. As the elevator lurched upward I tossed her a compliment. "Your coat is lovely."

Her eyes danced at me as she stroked the sable fur. "It was a gift from a client of mine." Her eyes moved up and down my tight jersey dress. The corners of her mouth turned up in a knowing smile. "Are you working today?"

I rolled my eyes. "Today and every day."

Opening her small bag she pulled out a card, handing it to me with a wink. "You can do better with my agency." She ran her hands down the lapel of her coat. "Who knows, maybe you'll earn one of these."

I choked back a retort before it could ruin my cover, then asked, "From the man you're seeing today?" She shook her head no as the eighth floor bell pinged and the doors opened. I moved past her and out of the view of the camera. I reached back for her card and quickly read the name. "Thank you, Candy." It was all I could do to keep myself from laughing at the ridiculous name. "I'll give them a call."

She winked at me again. "Please do. I get a finder's fee."

I held up my hand to wave, dumping my clutch and its contents all over the floor. "Sorry, I'm so clumsy." She stepped from the elevator to help me pick up my things. The moment the doors closed I pounced on her, knocking her out with little effort. "Sorry, Candy, but you're taking the night off."

I dragged her body to the maid's storage room and bound her with duct tape, covering her mouth so she couldn't scream when she woke. I stripped her of the black catsuit she was wearing, changing as quickly as possible and pulled on her coat for the finishing touch. Stepping over her body I offered, "Thank you again, do have a peaceful night." A thought occurred to me as I grasped the doorknob, causing me to turn and inspect Candy's hairline. Sure enough those blond tresses belonged to a wig. I braided my red hair quickly and secured the wig in place. At the elevator I checked the wig in my reflection and applied my peanut oil saturated lipstick. I looked myself in the eye and whispered, "Just in case he prefers blondes."

I got out on the ninth floor and started down the hallway as if I knew where I was going; soon two men came into view, pointing to my destination. I walked slowly to the room flirting with the taller of the two men. "Are you my date, handsome?"

His crooked smile swept over me. "No, but once you see my boss you'll wish I was." He nodded toward the other guard. "Hand him your purse."

I handed my clutch to the younger man to inspect while the taller opened my coat and ran his hands over my body. He didn't take his eyes from mine. As his hands reached my hips I said, "Careful, I'm not sure you can afford what you'll find there."

He smirked at my tease as the younger man handed him Candy's card. He moved closer to me. "We seem to have a problem." I raised my brows at him waiting for him to finish. He pushed me up against the wall his mouth close to mine. "You aren't Candy."

I leaned forward nibbling at his lower lip as I confirmed, "That's right. I'm sweeter than Candy and fresh." His eyes grew hungry. "If you can afford it, give my agency a call, ask for Blaze." Pressing my body into his, I moved toward the door. I took my clutch from the younger man holding the door open, brushing a finger along his jawline as I walked into the suite.

I followed the music till I found the old codger sprawled out on the bed wearing a hotel bathrobe. Swallowing down my disgust, I strolled closer as the fat man eyed me suspiciously. "I asked for Candy."

"I'm Blaze. The agency thought you might like to try their newest flavor." I let the heavy coat fall to the floor, revealing the skintight catsuit. "Trust me, I'm going to do something no other woman ever dared, something you'll remember for the rest of your life." His grin told me I said just the right thing. I closed the distance between us, jumping on the bed, towering over him in my thigh-high boots. Pushing my heel down on his chest I asked, "Shall we begin?"

He scowled up at me. "I'm not sure I like this game." He moved his hand to unzip my boot, "But let's see what your menu has to offer." I let him remove both of my boots then started dancing to the music, teasing him as I slowly removed the catsuit.

His eyes widened at the sight of my tattoo. He whistled softly, "I have never seen a tattoo like that before." I let him trace the tattoo from my ankle to my thigh, resisting the urge to pull away from his repulsive touch. "It's beautiful. Turn so I can see it all." His eyes followed the winding branch of the tree that wrapped my form from right toe to the right side of my neck. His finger outlined one of the petals as he said, "The pink is so vibrant." As I bent down intent of teasing him further he pulled me down to his chest, slamming his lips into mine, only to pull back quickly running his tongue over his lips. "Your lipstick taste strange." His shook his head, puzzled over the known but forgotten taste.

I giggled reaching for my purse to retrieve my weapon, a small bottle and then standing over him again to distract him from his thoughts. I unhooked my bra and dangled it above him till his eyes grew hungry once more. Smiling, I held up the small bottle of body oil and fluttered my eyes as I teased, "Do you like raspberries?" Not waiting for an answer I tossed the cork to the side and started pouring the lubricant over my chest. His eyes smoldered as I ran my hands through the oil on my body. I brought a finger up to my lips and sucked the oil off and whispered, "Want a taste?"

He pulled me back down to him with a growl, wildly licking my stomach making his way to my breast, sucking it and the oil in. I groaned in pretend pleasure. "Mmm, yeah lick me clean and then I get my turn with you." My promise drove him crazy and he darted for my other breast, frantic to get his turn in our little game.

My disgust meter was rising rapidly, threatening my cover, so I pushed him to his back and pulled open his bathrobe, winking at him as I poured the oil over his manhood. His smile faded as his hands flew to his throat, his face growing redder with each gasp of his straining lungs. Straddling his lap I smiled down at the gasping cheater, asking with a pout, "Want more baby?" I held his chin firmly, forcing his mouth open while pouring the remaining oil down his throat till nothing was left.

He thrashed wildly, trying to call out to his guards as the realization of what I was doing sunk in. I moaned and cried out to cover the noise he was making. When it was clear he was near the end I screamed as loud as I could to alarm the guards.

The two guards flew into the room. I pulled the sheet up to cover my body, pointing frantically at my blue-faced prey and screaming, "Help him!"

The tall guard took my elbow as the younger one knelt at the man's side. He stared down at me with furious eyes, demanding, "What happened?"

"I'm not sure." I pulled at my blond wig careful not to dislodge it, but enough to sell my performance. "We were having sex and he started turning color, I think he is having a heart attack." I screamed, "Call 9-1-1!" The young man obediently grabbed the phone and dialed.

The tall man turned his attention back to the bed and spotted the empty bottle of oil. "What is this?" He demanded as he reached for it.

"It's just raspberry-flavored body oil, I use it with all my clients." I made my eyes go wide as I did my best worried expression. "Is he going to be okay?"

He smelt the bottle then read the back of the label. "Oh my God, this is flavored peanut oil," he said as his eyes flew wide in my direction. I nodded my head yes. "You stupid bitch, he's allergic to peanuts."

"I didn't know, I'm so sorry," I stammered as I pushed forward, retrieving the bottle from his hands. "Does he carry an EpiPen?"

The younger man searched franticly for the life-saving injection, but the man's breathing was failing. I winked down at the old man so he would have no doubt I was the cause of his demise.

The senior partner pointed at me, grunting but unable to get words past his constricted airways. Misinterpreting, the tall man nodded at his boss. "I understand," he said as he grabbed my arm, pulling me from the bed. "Get dressed and get out of here, if he dies he doesn't want his wife to know you were here." I pulled on my coat as the guard shoved the rest of my clothes and boots into my arms. I made a show of staring dumbly at the body in its last throws of life. He shook me when I didn't move. "I said get out, and if anyone comes asking - you were never here." I ran from the room with a smile on my face...One down.

Back at the apartment I had acquired for this job, I grabbed a hot shower letting the water run down my face as I washed the last of the sticky oil from my body. With each drop of cleansing water, my call-girl persona circled the drain making way for the-girl-next-door persona to take effect for the next leg of this job. As I stepped from the shower the big brown eyes of Woodrow, a large Great Dane I had adopted for the junior partner portion of this assignment, reminded me he hadn't eaten breakfast yet. He followed me into the kitchen, waiting patiently as I set a small amount kibble in his empty dish. "Can't be too full this morning, boy, we have work to do," I said as I gave him an apologetic pat on his side.

If I hurried, I would have time for a quick bite as well before the junior partner's regular morning run. I figured that if I didn't act this morning I risked the chance they might double his guards when news of his partner's death reached his security team, or worse–lock him down completely. I left my hair in its still wet braid, stuffed it in a stocking hat and tossed in a pair of colored contacts. Satisfied with my makeover I headed for the breakfast diner near the park.

I was able to eat a relaxing meal while watching the sun peek up over the park. I threw the last bite of my three cheese omelet to Woodrow just as I spotted the junior partner's driver and quickly finished my cup of tea. I ruffled Woodrow's neck as I whispered, "You ready to do this?" We started jogging toward the park, wanting to be ahead of my victim on his route. Once in place I adjusted our pace to ensure we ended the run at the appropriate time. Woodrow and I were in place at the coffee cart just as my target's team come in view for the final part of his morning routine. I dropped to my knee, tying my shoelace allowing those behind me to move forward in line.

I stood reclaiming my place as he huffed his way in line behind me for his morning cup of coffee. I kept my eyes forward occasionally bending down to talk to Woodrow while waiting. When my turn came I placed my order and kept fiddling with the condiments, switching hands and position until I had Woodrow tangled in his leash. I sat my coffee on the counter and looked back at my target with an apologetic smile. "Sorry! I'll get out of your way in a moment."

He wrinkled up his nose at me, backing away from the large dog, clearly afraid of the close proximity. "No problem," he muttered as he held up one finger and called past me, "one Latte Macchiato." The vendor gave him a nod while I bent over Woodrow pretending to untangle his legs from the leash.

I pulled the small spray bottle from my pocket that Woodrow's trainer gave me coating my hands in the liquid he used when rewarding the dog. Woodrow caught the meaty scent and started drooling, trying to lap at my hands, twisting and turning as he attempted to claim his reward. I pushed my body forward tripping on the tight leash launching myself into my target's chest. I rubbed my hands all over his jogging suit as I apologized, "Oh no, I am so sorry." I fumbled awkwardly allowing one of his guards to help me up by my elbow. Falling down every chance I got until both guards were occupied helping me off their charge.

I let go of Woodrow's leash and he lunged forward at the man on the ground, pinning him down while he lapped and licked the reward covering the panic-stricken man. I called out, "Woodrow down." Not a command he was used to, the dog continued spreading his drool and making awful slurping sounds as he licked the juice off our victim's chest. One of the guards broke off to assist his charge but his sudden approach caused Woodrow to growl, driving our victim's panic further till I heard his breathing became raspy.

Then his breaths got shorter, followed by a wheezing sound, so I allowed myself to be stood upright. "I am so sorry," I said again. I gave my thigh a pat as I called the dog off. "Woodrow come!" The giant dog leapt off the junior partner and obediently trotted to my side. "I'm so sorry. Please let me pay for your dry cleaning," I stammered as I pulled the dog close to me, pretending to protect the man from further incident.

He sat up and waved his hand toward me motioning for me to stay away. "It's quite alright," he managed to say as he reached in his pocket, producing a small canvas bag and pulling out the inhalator I had sabotaged the night before. Between coughs he explained, "No harm done, I have asthma is all."

"I feel horrible," I said as I paid the vendor for his Macchiato. I shook my head at him when he tried to refuse. "It's the least I can do after my dog slobbered all over you, please." He nodded a thank-you at me as he took another puff of his inhaler. I smiled at him in sympathy. "Are you sure you will be alright?"

He took the hand of one of his guards and let them pull him to his feet. He brushed off his pants looking wearily at Woodrow and said, "Yes, thank you I'm fine." His breathing was less labored and the color was returning to his face. He had no idea of the inherent danger now lurking within his body. Most likely it wouldn't be discovered for a few days, by then my dog and I would be a distant memory. I almost felt sorry for him till the faces of his victims crossed my mind and I let justice push my guilt away.

A guard stepped forward, insisting, "I think it would be best if you took your dog and left."

I tossed the man one last fake apologetic look and jogged off with Woodrow at my side. I reached down and scratched behind his ears. "Great job, partner, time will do the rest and fate will determine if he lives or dies. Either way room has been made for our operative to move into position, so my job is done."

CHAPTER •———— TWO

He frowned as he glanced up from the body lying on his table, spotting me in the corner waiting my turn. With a heavy sigh he asked, "Why do you always come when I'm booked solid?"

I folded my arms and leaned against the wall. "That hurts my feelings, Kenji. Would you rather I didn't come at all?"

He sighed again. "No." Kenji gave the man on his table a slap on the back then said, "Something has come up we'll have to reschedule."

His customer arched his back, looking over his shoulder at the nonexistent tattoo on his calf. "You haven't even started," he huffed.

Kenji gave him another shove and insisted, "Just go. I'll finish it for half price later." Irritated at being forced to discount his work Kenji started cleaning his tools. He called for his assistant, "Dani!"

The dissatisfied patron glared at me. "My money spends the same as hers and I was here first." He sprawled over the table and grunted. "Finish my tat, the redhead can wait her damned turn."

Kenji's eyes narrowed on his customer, his words dripping with disdain. "First of all I don't do tats, I am *hiro* and my work is art." I took a step forward but Kenji's eyes begged me to stop as he shook his head slightly. "Second, I am under contract, buddy, so you have to go."

When Kenji's assistant rounded the corner her eyes went wide when they met mine, the tray she held clattered to the floor. "You!"

I smiled, trying to calm her down, but I couldn't suppress my mirth and a half-laugh made its way out as I asked, "This is your new assistant, Ji?" Kenji's lips thinned out as he held in his irritation. Attempting to make peace for Kenji's sake, I held out my hand and offered an apology. "I am sorry about what happened last time we met." She shrank from my hand, recalling the last time it was offered. Both Dani and the customer began talking over one another competing for Kenji's attention till the room was nothing but a dull roar.

"Stop!" Kenji yelled. He winced in pain at the sound then whispered, "You're giving me a migraine." He turned toward me, his eyes pleading with me to understand as he spoke, "You have to quit doing this to me, Red. What are we doing this time?"

I took a deep breath and answered despite the other two glaring at me. "Five flowers and a bird. I'll be gone before you know it."

Kenji pulled the hand towel from the sink basin wringing the cloth in his hands. He looked intently at his customer and lied, "I have an arrangement with a local...umm... club of sorts. They provide me protection and I cover their ink. I can't afford to insult their club president's old lady. Give me a few hours and I will finish dropping your ink later tonight." The man continued to grumble but got up and left without further incident.

"You're actually going to work on this bitch?" Dani was frantic and I realized her tone could only mean they were sleeping together. "The last time she was here she put me through the front window. Or don't you remember inking over my scars?"

I shrugged and muttered, "I said I was sorry."

I curled my lip when Kenji glared at me. "Red that isn't helping." He took Dani's hands in his and lowered his tone as he said, "I explained that she was dangerous and you wouldn't stop." He shook his head when her eyes widened in disbelief and continued, "I am not saying what she did was right, or that is was your fault, but we talked about this. You know I can't turn her away, now go rearrange my appointments."

"Fine." She glared at me with jealous eyes. "But I'm not coming back till she's gone."

After she stomped from the room I walked toward the table, eyebrows raised. "You told her I was dangerous?"

"Hardly a secret, given you threw her through a window." He huffed the words out at me. He didn't look up from the pigments he was mixing when he asked, "All pink or do we have another white?"

I clenched my jaw down as I forced out the words, "There won't ever be another white." The memory of the one innocent life I took flooded my mind. I shook my head clear of the big brown eyes that often haunted my dreams. "I thought I asked you not to bring that up again. In fact, I know I did." I slipped from my clothes, covering myself with a sheet from the shelf. "Ji, I can't come back here again. Too many people have seen me."

"And I can't move again. My business is finally making money and...things have changed," he stammered. He spun around and blurted out, "I asked Dani to marry me. She doesn't know anything about Japan or you, and I plan to keep it that way." He peeked at me from the corner of his eye. "You know I won't tell anyone anything even if they lock me up or kill me. You got my dad and me out of Japan." He motioned toward the table as he said, "I owe you my life, but I'm not moving again. We have to make other arrangements from now on. You aren't exactly a people person and you seem hell bent on making a scene every time you show up."

I frowned and sighed, "I don't do it on purpose."

"Right." He snorted. "You could have fooled me." A red silk bag revealed his bamboo needles, which he handled with loving care. "Could we set a date, time and place for your next session or could you at least give me some type of notice?" He pored over my skin trying to decide the best placement of these tattoos as they were added to his showpiece. "Or are you finally getting out of the business, and these are the last petals I will be doing for you?"

I smirked at his hidden agenda. "Ji, someone has to keep the world safe. I am good at my job and frankly what else would I do?"

"I don't know, maybe get married and have a couple of kids?" He started outlining on my thigh as he offered. "You know, do what normal people do, fall in love."

I took a deep breath. "I would be a terrible mother, Ji, and an even worse wife." I shook my head at the thought. "I'll send you a location, date, and time for next time, but you cannot breathe a word to anyone. not even your little Dani."

He gave my thigh a swat to make his point and said, "You know I won't."

Kenji got to work while I thought about the file that Conrad had retrieved as the promised reward for the Texas job. It's strange how you can feel directionless right after you achieve a goal, as if your mind can't grasp what you achieved. I was so close to my final goal I should have been elated, but I felt emptier than ever. All that was left was to study my enemy, develop a plan, and wreak my vengeance. My team would have justice, even if our government forced me to do it myself. Hell, it was our own people that sent us in there to die.

After begging me not to hold him responsible, Conrad handed over the file. The shame on his face prepared me the truth. Our agency used this group of mercenaries to scrub their unwanted teams by setting up missions that were doomed to fail. Their Mexico base of operations was dug into a mountainside and the only known entrance was heavily fortified. Without inside information and careful planning it was, at best, a suicide mission. I let out a sigh of irritation.

"Did I hurt you, or are you having another private conversation with yourself?"

I shot him an annoyed glare and answered, "Think you know me do you?" He smiled up at me and my heart broke at the sight. All the faces of those I had dared let into my heart flooded my mind. Even Woodrow's brown eyes stared back at my soul when I returned him after securing that weapons shipment in Texas. But how could I care for him with my lifestyle? It's doubtful I'll even live through what's coming next. "Don't start to like me, Ji. Everyone who has ever cared about me is dead." I turned my head and plopped it back down on the table to hide my unspent tears.

"That isn't true, Red. You're family to me, and I am alive." He shrugged. "Okay, maybe family you never knew you had, and that you have no idea where they live now, but you are still the closest thing I have to family left in this world."

"Lucky you," I muttered.

"Yes, lucky me," he whispered. "You know I thought I was dead for sure. I'll never forget the look on my father's face when he shoved me into the closet and told me my mother and brother had been murdered. He buried me under clothes and shoes and demanded I stay there as long as I could no matter what I heard or saw and above all else not to make a sound."

"I am sorry you lost your family, Ji. I was too slow to save your mother and brother."

He huffed out his breath, "See? Even now you shoulder the blame, as if any of it was yours to bear. We should have died. When an *oyabun* gives an order, it is carried out."

"They found your body. As long as you stay off their radar, you are dead," I whispered. I tried to change the subject. "Although I do wish you had chosen a different profession. Your work is too distinct; someone could recognize your father's techniques."

Kenji pulled on my hip, rolling me to my side so he could finish the last flower on my inner thigh. His lips twisted around his words, "It should be enough that I cannot use my father's name, or be known as *hiro* at all. I don't use my needles on anyone but you. I won't let them take everything from my family; our art is all that is left now that my father has passed. I must honor my father and pass it down to my children, along with the truth of their heritage." He stared, unmoving till I turned and met his gaze. "All of it."

<hr>

I pulled up to the tiny inn that my team had used the last time we came down to Mexico, the final time we went anywhere together. The jolly innkeeper rolled out of the doorway with a smile as he greeted me. "Back to climb our mountains I see." Diego bounded toward the Jeep to collect my bags. "Let me grab the gear, if it's as heavy as last time, you should have your friends pack it in." He frowned as he looked down at the three heavy bags then asked, "Are you by yourself *senorita*?"

"Yes, my two friends weren't able to make it this

trip." It wasn't a lie. I held back the rest of what was going through my mind. After all it wasn't his fault that the hills held a band of ruthless killers, he probably had to live with the fear of them every day.

He shook his head and held his hands out to me as he emphatically said, "You go home. It's not safe to be here without men. You are too pretty, *pequeña,* to be alone in our mountains."

I smiled at his concern. "You know us crazy Americans. We just can't stop when we get an idea in our head." I tilted my head at him when he moved to put my bag back in the Jeep. "I'll be fine, I promise. I won't go far and I will be back every night before dark."

Diego let out a heavy sigh as he grabbed my bags, mumbling something in Spanish so quickly I couldn't understand as he led me into the sparsely lit room that served as the local watering hole. He was still grumbling to himself as we climbed the stairs to my room. Tossing the bags down on the bed, he spun around and shook a finger at me demanding, "Home before dark! Come down when you are ready for dinner, my wife made you that chili you like and fresh tortillas."

I smiled trying to hide my shock at their vivid memories of my first trip here. "Tell Elena I said thank you for remembering, and that I will be down in about twenty minutes. I just need to settle in." With a nod, he turned and left my room, still mumbling under his breath. My room was at the end of the hall as I requested. It was the easiest to defend with only the door and one window and gave me time to hear someone's approach from the hall. It wasn't like me to return to the same place and use the passport from a previous mission, but coming back as the same person made me feel as if I was clearing the slate. It would feel like true justice, and since my cover hadn't been blown, I didn't see the harm.

Only the agency had known we were here, but they never knew what passports we traveled under. We always booked separate flights, never traveling together and were rarely on the same flight. I'm sure their deaths were never reported to the Mexican authorities, they simply disappeared. I took one last look at my passport, October Jenkins. That had been Mace's doing. I smirked to myself as I let memories of him flood over me. He was always giving me crazy names, I am sure at one time or another I had been every month in the year, even a planet or two. I buried my passport in a drawer under my under garments then quietly moved the dresser and taped my secondary passport to the backside with duct tape.

I set up my alarm wire to the window and

finished by hiding two pistols - one by the bed and one in the bathroom. Tossing the roll of duct tape into my bag I surveyed the room one final time before I was satisfied with my prep work. Tonight I will slip out the window and scout for a suitable interrogation spot. Tomorrow my work would begin.

Elena was waiting at the end of the stairs with a warm smile and a greeting of her own. "Welcome back, *hermoso fuego*," she said as she pulled me into the dining room.

My face must have been blank as I heard a man chuckle from the corner table. He lifted a glass at me, offering a translation. "It means beautiful fire."

I felt my cheeks burning from the compliment. "Thank you," I answered. I took the table next to his, as it was the only empty one in the back of the room.

He leaned forward and said, "You may join me if you like. The room fills up fast here when the lumberworkers get off shift. That is, unless you have someone joining you." He sat back in his chair pushing his empty plate forward before he fished further. "Your husband, perhaps?"

I ignored his probing question and answered, "Thank you, but I'm fine right here. I won't be staying long."

Elena returned with a large bowl and a plate of

tortillas. "Nice and thick, just as you like it. I made you *alegrias* for a snack later. Shall I put them in your room?"

"No, Elena, I will grab them on my way up, and thank you for thinking of me."

"Oh, yes, I forgot you don't want me to service your room during your stay. I will put fresh bedding out every three days like last time." I nodded in appreciation of her memory, though I must have interacted with her too often on our former trip for her to recall me so vividly. Was I that sloppy? She smiled widely at me, tilting her head slightly in the direction of the man at the next table. "I see you have met our Don Alejandro Galinez."

I offered a half smile and tried to be polite. "Not formally, but yes we have spoken."

"Don Alejandro, this is Señora October. She comes down to climb our mountains." She winked at me and said, "Don Alejandro owns a *hacienda grande* nearby and comes to visit us often to ensure we are doing well."

I felt my face flush deeper. I was receiving entirely too much unwanted attention. Confused by all the mistakes I was making, I found myself at a loss for words. The dark-haired man came to my rescue. "Elena, your *birria* was fantastic as always.

Will you make me a Tequila Fuego in honor of your lovely guest?"

She smiled and excused herself. I thought he would try to make further conversation but he surprised me with peaceful silence. The room started to fill up, thankfully keeping Elena busy. I watched the room, regretting that there was no other place to eat in town, and that Elena did not allow meals to be served in the rooms. Perhaps I could get her to pack all my meals to go.

I allowed myself to examine the man next to me with my peripheral vision. Fair skin, dark wavy hair and penetrating blue eyes – coupled with his accent his origins were definitely in Spain. He carried himself confidently and seemed comfortable with his own company. And something else I couldn't quite put my finger on, I felt drawn to him. Charisma? No, something far more dangerous – attraction. I ate quicker than normal as I felt his eyes inspecting me from time to time.

By the time Elena returned with his drink I had devoured my meal. She frowned at me in disapproval. "You should not eat so fast."

"Then you shouldn't cook so well." My comment was rewarded with a wide smile. "Can I get those *alegrias* now? I am exhausted from my trip and I want to hit the mountains early, so perhaps you could pack my breakfast?" She tossed me a nod, scampering off with my bowl and I stood to go.

"You are very kind, for an American," the dark haired man called out. I turned slightly to shift my eyes to his and he tipped his glass to me.

I stared at him for a moment before I said, "I don't believe I have ever been referred to as kind." Squaring my shoulders I looked him in the eyes and said flatly, "Let me be blunt, just in case Elena's matchmaking has given you any ideas. I'm not interested." Anger rushed through me as the corners of his mouth lifted in a slight smile. "In fact, it would be better for you to forget you ever met me."

I woke to the vibration of my watch alarm. It was barely dusk - perfect for my scouting trip. I braided my hair tight to my head and slipped into my gear before I crawled out the window to the roof. There was still enough light to easily make my way through the alleys between the small wood cabins. I needed to find a secure and isolated spot for my coming interrogations, I couldn't risk being found, or this trip would end far too soon.

On our previous trip we set up in a small abandoned brewery, but I was leery of making use of it as I was already taking too many risks with repeat behavior. And it was too close to town, someone would surely hear if things got out of hand. Still with a town this size, I didn't have a lot of options. I was about to turn back to the brewery when I spotted a large dark roofline roughly two klicks north of town. I climbed to a higher elevation and zoomed in on the shape with my scope. No sign of activity. I switched sensors, but found no heat signature. It was worth a closer look.

I kept to the shadows as I approached. This area gave me the creeps and I kept feeling as though I was being watched. I doubled back, scouting for any sign of counter surveillance, but found nothing. By the time I reach my goal, night was fully upon me, I cussed myself out for only bringing the night scope and not a set of goggles. I would have to risk a light, telling myself it would be a good test of privacy. If I was discovered I would ditch my gear and pretend to be lost.

I turned on my flashlight and thought I saw darkness skitter away on my right, too large to be a rat. I cut the light and searched through my scope, but again came up empty handed. My mind had to be playing tricks on me. I popped my light on and searched the empty home room by room – no one had lived here in years. The only furniture that wasn't broken or rotted was an oversized wooden chair. "The guy that lived here must have fancied himself some small town kingpin with a throne such as this," I mumbled to myself. I pushed the throne-like chair, but it only groaned at my efforts. Well that solves that, the only reason it was still here is it was too heavy to cart off. "I can use you." I nodded to the large chair. "Yes, you will work just fine."

I prepped the room to the best of my ability with the materials I salvaged, nailing up the rotten mattresses that I found upstairs and various cushions in an attempt to halfway soundproof the room. I pulled up a few floorboards and stashed Axe's pain kit. I never cared for torture, but the file detailed the group's fierce devotion to their unknown leader, so I was left no other option. I would keep the last images of Mace and Axe in the forefront of my mind for motivation to get what I needed out of my victim. Tomorrow, I would hunt.

CHAPTER ●———THREE

At daybreak, I was ready to go, decked out in brown, grey and green, the best I could do without dressing in camouflage. I tucked my braid in a stocking hat, picked up my gear and slipped downstairs. As promised, Elena had a package waiting for me in the kitchen. I grabbed it hurrying out to avoid being caught and forced into conversation.

Diego was leaning against a post on the porch talking to someone as I made my way outside. I heard him say, "The blood drive is tonight."

"The thought disgusts me," the man they called Don Alejandro replied. I watched him motion in my direction signaling to Diego they were not alone. His blue eyes were spellbinding in the morning light, making it difficult not to return his smile. "Morning, Miss. October," he said with a slight nod of his head.

"Good morning," I replied abruptly. Moving past them I tossed my gear in the back of the Jeep.

He followed me, then leaned against my wheel well, looking down at me with those intense blue eyes and said, "I would open your door like a gentleman, but somehow I doubt you would take that as a compliment."

His crooked smile made my stomach flip. Caught off-guard by my attraction I tried to hide my interest with a snide comment. "Can you get your ass off my Jeep?" Immediately, I regretted being rude. I couldn't wrap my mind around why I kept acting this way; October was a happy-go-lucky hiker. I could blow my cover. "Sorry, it's a long way to where I want to climb today, and I'm burning daylight. I didn't mean to be rude."

"Apparently you didn't get your coffee this morning," he said as his smile moved to his eyes. Despite my instincts screaming a warning, I smiled at his remark and allowed him to open my door without protest. Closing the door after I got in, he leaned forward and asked, "Do you need a climbing partner? I could re-arrange my schedule, if you like."

My heart skipped a beat and I blinked back my surprise at the offer. "Umm, thank you but I came down to work out some personal issues, and to do that I need alone time. Besides, I don't climb with strangers."

"I can understand that," he said with a wink. "But I'll be in town a few days if you change your mind. Perhaps I can persuade you to become an acquaintance."

I couldn't hold back the smile his offer brought to my lips. "I'll keep that in mind." His eyes were fixed on me as I put the Jeep in reverse and headed out. He raised a hand to say good-bye and I watched him wave till he faded out of my rearview mirror.

***

Today's destination was several miles northwest from the logging camp. I had to hike in or risk being seen as they were set up in an old cliff-side monastery. A single road led straight to the fortress and they had cleared most of the surrounding vegetation to ensure visibility, so their leader's understanding of strategy wasn't to be underestimated.

I set a brisk pace, making great time locating the surveillance blind we had used on our last trip, and quickly repaired the damage wind and hard rains had wrought in our absence. Images and memories surfaced of Mace and Axe while I put my hands to task. I smiled as I recalled Mace and me being disgusted at Axe's inability to tolerate Elena's spicy food.

"What?" Axe stared back at us, trying to look innocent.

My eyes rolled back into my head and I tried to shake the imaginary green fog from around my vicinity. "Honestly, Axe, that is horrible."

Mace whispered, "God you're toxic! You forgot to bring Beano down with you, didn't you?"

Axe's sides heaved in repressed laughter as he choked out a reply, "I can't help it."

I quietly coughed, "Oh my God...it's in my mouth." I grabbed the canteen, pulling a long drink. Then I gargled and spit out the last of the water in an effort to free my taste buds from his rancid odor.

A grimace transformed Mace's features till he was coughing as well. Kicking his still laughing brother, he whispered, "It smells like something crawled up there and died." When Axe let out more gas with a chuckle, Mace punched his brother in the side. "You pig, at least go downwind if you have to do that again or I'll kick your ass."

Axe smiled, refocused his sights on his scope, and whispered a warning, "Keep hitting my stomach and you'll get another dose."

I sat there for what seemed like forever missing Mace's patience for surveillance and struggling with my irritation at having to do his job. The camp was dead quiet, just as Mace had forewarned. He had discovered that the camp was most active after sunset. We figured it was some misplaced effort to avoid satellite detection. It just goes to show how little criminals know, night often brought us some of the clearest intelligence, as most people let their guard down under the cover of darkness.

They had been busy repairing the damage I had left during my last exit; only a few structures still bore the scars of my rage. I glanced down at the silent vibration of my watch signaling yet another hour had passed; the sun was setting and there had been zero activity. I could see why Mace had made the choice to get a closer look. The camp seemed devoid of life, not even a chicken or stray dog crossed my sights. I forced my body to stay still, ignoring the sporadic cramps in my legs, trying to see the camp through Mace's eyes, tracing with my mind the possible route he would have chosen before he moved in and went missing. His death had proven the mercs have eyes hidden in the shadows of the compound. To succeed, I cannot make the same mistakes; I will have to force myself to be patient.

Behind those clay walls lay an unknown threat lurking in a cave system carved out by long gone zealot monks. There were no blueprints to study, no information on the numbers I faced, no intel on the training this group has been given, or the weapons waiting to greet me. "And no team to cover my flank," I whispered. I was truly alone. Sure, Conrad knew I was making this attempt, but we both knew my chances of getting out of this alive were slim to none. "He's probably dancing on my fake grave." I scoffed at the image.

Finally, just inside the shadow of the cliff side, as the last rays of daylight ebbed, I caught movement -

a single sentry. I adjusted my scope, focusing in on a scrawny frame making what appeared to be a half-assed effort at a perimeter check. I scanned the camp for any other movement. I pulled the lens down, stunned at the thoughts I was having at attempting this snatch and grab without further recon. Another scan came up empty except for the single man halfway through his walk of the perimeter.

I quickly ran through the scenario in my head. I had plenty of time to get into position before he doubled back. True, dragging him through the brush to where I had the Jeep parked would slow me down, but he was a runt of a man, so it shouldn't be much of a problem. My dart gun was loaded before I realized I had made the decision to move. I threw the rope over my shoulder and rushed the wall, staying as low as possible, positioning myself to intercept him on his return trip.

Not only was he frail looking, but he was slow as a snail. I sent up a silent prayer that the dose of tranquilizer I was using wouldn't kill him. Time ticked by, my nerves were near their limit by the time he came into view. My heart thundered in my ears as he approached. I hated using tranquilizers, every person reacted differently, and I needed to get him out without raising an alarm. I pushed down my fear of being caught, took a deep breath, and pulled the trigger.

He didn't cry out like I thought he would, simply swatted at his neck until he sunk to the ground in a groggy heap. I leapt out from cover, cinching up his legs in a tight knot then shoving a cloth down his throat securing it in place with duct tape. I dragged his body from the compound to the cover of the sparse brush line as fast as I could, then scrambled up the blind to see if anyone was on our trail. With no one in sight and no apparent alarms triggered, I allowed myself to let out a breath of relief.

In the cover of the clump of thicker brush, I rechecked my bound prey. He started to struggle against the ropes. Confused, I shook my head and whispered, "I know I gave you too large of a dose for your size already." I reached for my tackle box and produce another dose of tranquilizer. "Just to be safe," I said as I shoved the needle under his skin. "After all, I can't have you struggling against me while I'm packing you out to the road."

I loaded up my remaining gear then rolled my prisoner onto the makeshift stretcher and started out for the Jeep. I could not believe my luck. Lost in thoughts of my incredibly fast success, I wasn't paying attention to the load I was dragging behind me till I felt the weight drastically change. My head spun around and I caught him trying to drag his still bound body back toward the compound, one inch at a time.

"What the hell!" There was a lot of fight left in him so I grabbed another dose. He struggled against me as I readied the shot, dislodging his gag in the process. I snarled at him. "At this rate I'll be out of tranqs before I get you there." As his eyes rolled back into his head, I shook my head at him in wonder and demanded, "How are you burning through these drugs? I gave you enough to put an elephant down."

He pulled back his lips in a drugged sneer, "Let me go, Bitch!"

I threw my head back and laughed as I slammed his face into the ground for good measure and said, "Good! You speak English. That will make my job easier."

He was dead weight the rest of the trip, making lifting him into the Jeep a chore. Still, it was better than having him struggling against me. I just hoped that I hadn't overdosed him; it would be a pity to waste this opportunity.

I pulled his body into the house, letting his head bounce up the steps as I rushed to get him secured before he woke up again. I pulled the ropes tight to his chest and wrapped them around the chair not caring if they cut into his skin. A smile touched my lips. He won't live through this, a fact I have to keep to myself. Captives don't tend to give up information if they think there's no chance they'll walk away with their lives.

Just as I finished securing his legs his head rolled back. Astounded, I watched as he started coming to yet again. "What kind of drugs are you on?" I slammed his head against the chair and forced an eyelid open. "How the hell are you burning off these tranquilizers so quickly?" His pupil registered on me. "I see you are awake." Ripping off the last strip of duct tape from the roll, I backed away from him shoving the rag in my pocket. "Good. We can begin earlier than I expected. I have a few questions for you and then you can go back to your friends."

"Let me go and I won't kill you," he snarled.

I huffed back a laugh. "You aren't going anywhere until you answer my questions."

His eyes narrowed in anger. Growling at me he began struggling against the ropes till one around his chest began to fray from the strain. Shocked, I ran for my bag quickly ripping back the edge of a new roll of duct tape. I tightly wound the tape around his chest from shoulder to elbow and didn't stop until there was no sign of movement in his torso. I followed suit with each limb and then for good measure I taped his forehead to the back of the thick throne.

I smiled down at him as he strained against the unmoving duct tape. "Perhaps now you'll behave!" He struggled against the rope and tape till he realized his body was practically glued to the heavy chair. I circled him, poking and prodding him in random places. "You're pretty strong for a man with such a skinny frame."

"And you're dead!"

I put my hand to my chest in fake innocence. "Really?" Wide eyed I shoved my fingers to my jugular vein exhaling dramatically in relief. "Nope, still pumping." I laughed as he bared his teeth at me in rage. "You, on the other hand, may not be alive much longer if you don't settle down and answer a few questions."

I circled him again, ticking off my questions. "How many men are at your compound? Is there another entrance? What kind of weapons do the men have? Are there patrols inside the compound? If so, what is the rotation schedule?" I stopped in front of him, leaning down to look into his hazel eyes. "Answer these simple questions and after I have killed all your friends I will allow you to live and go free."

He smiled and offered, "If you wanted to meet the men, all you had to do was ask." His smile widened. "I could take you there for dinner and you can get all the answers you want first hand."

I slid my fingers down his cheek and lowered my voice, "The thought of seduction did cross my mind." Leaning in I whispered in his ear, "Is that what you want?" I let my breath travel down his neck as my hand slid down his chest toward his beltline. "A little pleasure and you would give me the answers I seek?" I looked down at his pants, gnawing on my lip at the reaction my words were having on his manhood. I knelt down in front of him, waiting for an answer.

"They aren't my friends anyway, kill them all. I'll even help you," he said in a low rumble. "Let me go and I'll help you."

I caressed his thigh peeking up at him through my lashes. "Is that all it would take for you to take my side?"

"I said they aren't my friends. I don't like a single one of them."

I shoved my hand in between his legs, latching onto what I found there and twisting with all my strength. "What a pathetic liar."

He screamed out in pain. "You bitch!"

"Thank you. I needed to see what you look like when you lie, now we're ready to begin."

Unmoved by my threat he closed his eyes and chortled. "I'm going to kill you slowly, savoring my time with you."

I raised an eyebrow, having never encountered this reaction from a captive. "Normally I would have taken time to watch you, and would have discovered your propensity for delusions. Are you on medication?" He couldn't hold back his sneer, but kept his eyes closed pretending to ignore me. I let out a sigh. "Not interested in what I am about to do to you?"

He opened his eyes, peered up at me and said, "Every minute you keep me here I will repay with an hour of my own torture."

I smiled at him and chuckled back. "Keep telling yourself that, if it makes you feel better." Pulling up the floor boards I retrieved Axe's pain kit, tossing it down on a rickety table with a thud. "Axe was our extractor, but I know enough to get what I want from you without too much effort."

"You don't have the balls for serious torture, you're just a girl."

I opened the bag, unfazed by his chauvinistic rattling. "It's true I don't really enjoy torture, but in your case I'll make an exception." I pulled the table closer so he could see the items I laid out. "For your part in the killing of my team, I am going to make you beg me to kill you, how's that for 'just a girl'?"

"You can't kill me, bitch." He laughed.

Finished emptying the bag's contents, I tossed the bag aside. "That's what I do. I kill people and I'm good at my job."

"So, you're an assassin that's pissed off we killed someone trying to kill us?"

"Basically, but the difference is the people I kill deserve it. It's justified. What you do is for greed and power. We're nothing alike." I pulled off my brown hoody, tossing it to the ground and shoved my hands down into my boots, pulling out my brass knuckles. I circled his chair sliding the knuckles along the tape as I walked. "I didn't get a chance to work out today, so if you don't mind, we'll get that out of the way first."

I pounded on him repeatedly, not asking any questions, simply working out my anger at the loss of my friends. I worked the length of his body trying to avoid breaking too many bones, but regretting I hadn't thought of suspending him like a punching bag. Seething eyes followed me during my assault; his refusal to cry out in pain fueling my anger.

An hour later, sweat dripped from my body almost as abundant as the blood ran from his wounds. I was so spent I could barely lift my arms. I drove my fist into his jaw one last time, asking, "Who's the bitch now?"

The beating had loosened the tape job, allowing his head to hang slightly. I rinsed my favorite pair of brass knuckles in the bucket of water one by one, examining the bruises they had inflicted on my hands.

His battered lips smirked at me as he spit a mouthful of blood on the floor in front of me. "Feel better?" If his eyes weren't so swollen I would have sworn he winked at me.

"I haven't even gotten started." Placing a hand on either arm of his chair I leaned in asking, "How many men are at your compound?"

"Enough to kick your tiny ass," he said as he lunged forward, snapping at me with his teeth.

I let out a deep sigh as I pulled myself upright and out of the way of his attack. "I see." Moving to the table I retrieved the roll of tape. As I worked on re-enforcing his bonds, I asked, "Do you know there are roughly two hundred and six bones in the human body?" I jabbed my fingers into his ribs, receiving a snarling scream for my pleasure. "I'm pretty sure I have broken at least two of your ribs already." I smiled down at him and asked, "How many more shall I break until you answer my questions?"

His eyes rolled wildly at me. "I'm not telling you anything," he answered.

Running my fingers over his, I continued, "The hand alone has twenty-seven bones, not including your sesamoid bones, which vary between people." Taking a deep breath I traced the back on his hand. "The human body is remarkable, it starts healing the moment it's injured." I flashed him a sinister smile and said, "That means I could break your bones and they would start repairing themselves, and we could start all over in a few days. I will break and re-break till there's not much the doctors can do to repair the damage; of course you will fade in and out of consciousness making it hard to get the answers I seek." I brushed my fingertips gently against his blood-soaked face and said, "But I'm willing to play if you are."

"I'm not telling you shit!" He spat.

"Tsk, tsk. If you insist on doing this the hard way, I guess I'll have to indulge your masochistic desires, but remember you brought this on yourself." Pulling the cloth from my pocket, I shoved it deep in his mouth despite his efforts to bite my fingers. "I know how dedicated you are to your boss, so I won't bother asking you a question after each broken bone. I'm going to start with your left hand and I'll ask one question after...what do you say, every other bone?" The cloth muffled his retort but his good eye glared at me in hatred. "Third?" He continued to glare, shaking his head. "Three it is."

Picking up the hammer from the table I tapped it against my palm. "Don't worry, I am schooled in anatomy, I'll do my best to minimize the nerve damage." I rolled my eyes and teased, "Well, I mean I'll save that for later." I let the hammer hover over his hand and called out, "Eenie- meenie-miney-mo, catch a killer by the toe, if he talks let him go. My hammer picks which phalange to break and you are it." I slammed the hammer down on the tip of his ring finger hearing the crunch just before his muffled scream. "Twenty-six to go," I winked at him and started my rhyme again. After breaking the tips of his thumb and pinky I asked, "How many men are at your compound?"

As I pulled the rag from his mouth he spit at me but refused to mutter a word. "Well that isn't very smart," I said as I wiped the spit from my arm. "I'm not going to give you any water till you give me something useful, so you should conserve your moisture." Gagging him again, I started my rhyme.

I took my time inflicting as much psychological damage as possible during my quest for information, but he proved loyal to his comrades, not answering a single question. His body was limp, broken, and bleeding, but his will was strong and unyielding. Only six bones remained unbroken in his left hand, but it was clear this was getting me nowhere. I pulled the blood-soaked rag from his mouth and asked once more, "How many men are at the compound?"

His head rolled up allowing him to glare at me from a half closed lid. "My master will bleed you dry for this," he said with a curled lip.

"Master? You call your boss, 'Master'?" I fought to hold in my laughter but choked out, "Who in the hell calls someone 'master' in this day and age?" Mocking him, I wiggled my head back and forth calling, "Master, master, the bad lady took me hostage."

Growling he lunged forward rocking the massive chair. "You're..."

I cut him off holding up my hand. "No, let me guess. I'm dead!" I chuckled at the hate in his eyes as I continued to mock him, "Your master is going to kill me for harming his precious runt." Smiling, I bent down looking him in the eye. "No, little one, it is I who will kill your master and every last criminal lurking in your lair. It's time to pay for slaughtering my team. You can either tell me what I need to know and live. Or you can die and I'll go get a replacement. Sooner or later one of you will tell me what I need to know to take down your little operation."

"You have no idea what's coming for you." He spit. "When they realize I'm missing, you're going to pay."

I drove my hammer into his knee, smiling at him as he released a hair-raising shriek. Turning toward the table I sighed. "Well this isn't having the desired effect, so let's try something else. Perhaps this?" I spun around, showing him the thin blade of a filet knife. "This belonged to Axe." My lips twisted at the memory of my teammates. "I think it's only fitting he's represented at our little party. I once watched Axe peel the skin off a drug dealer's hand with this blade, he kept it razor sharp."

"Your pathetic attempts to scare me mean nothing, you can't kill me."

Resisting the urge to shove the blade in his gut, I snapped, "Make no mistake I can and will kill you if you don't give me the information I want." His cocky smirk got the better of me and I slid the blade across his bicep thankfully missing an artery and not dislodging my tape job.

He drew in his breath as the knife parted his flesh and the blood streamed down his arm. His tongue jutted out for the gushing wound like a dog. "You bitch!"

"How many men are at the compound?"

He snarled, "When my master returns, you will pay for this!"

The small victory brought a smile to my lips as I said, "So the compound is without its leader. Now see, that wasn't so hard was it? For a reward I'll give you a drink." Grabbing a bottle of water I twisted off the cap, offering him a sip. "You must be thirsty."

As I brought the bottle to his lips he snapped at my wrist with his teeth and whispered, "You have no idea."

Barely pulling my hand back in time I rewarded his attack with a left hook. "Are you just stupid or do you have a death wish?" I threw the water in his face. "There's your water. Let's start again, how many men are left at the compound?" When he refused to answer I slid my knife across the back of his hand. Again and again I slashed my way up his arm till I reached his shoulder. Still he refused to answer my questions. I watched the blood flow down his arm staining the duct tape deep red. "At this rate you'll bleed out and I'll be forced to gather one of your friends to answer my questions."

"You will bleed out at my feet." He sneered.

"You want more blood, huh?" Careful not to nick the femoral artery I leaned in, slicing his thigh open.

A low guttural groan escaped his bloodless lips along with a threat, "I'm going to force you to watch me kill everyone you have ever loved before I drain the life from your body."

"Your team already did!" I grabbed the bottle of rubbing alcohol from the table slicing the lid off, then towered over him drenching his wounds and watching him dance under its blistering touch. His screams did nothing to quell my anger. "I'll give you a chance to think about answering my questions," I said as I retrieved the empty canvas bag and shoved it over his head so he could sweat out the night. "I'll be back later to give you one last chance to save your life." I paused at the door, calling out over my shoulder, "Try not to bleed out before I get back."

It was well after dark by the time I pulled up to the lodge, my clothes clinging to me in the Mexican night air while my stomach growled from all the calories I had burned off in my torture session. I lingered behind the wheel, content to sit in silence for a moment watching the abnormally busy street.

A white-paneled van was parked across the street from the cantina with a long line of people stringing out behind it. Then I recalled Diego's words from the morning regarding a blood drive. I shook my head at the turn out muttering to myself, "I didn't think that many people called this place home."

Feeling eyes on me, I scanned my mirrors, trying to locate the source. It appeared clear, but my instincts rarely fail me and I couldn't shake the feeling that someone had been shadowing me. I shook off my suspicions, convincing myself I was hyperaware since losing Mace and Axe. Still I would have to double my counter surveillance to be safe.

The blood drive provided just the distraction I needed to slip in undetected. Craving a shower more than food, and wanting to avoid answering questions about my blood-stained appearance, I took the steps two at a time. I checked the hair I left in my door before entering. Finding it undisturbed, I smirked at my paranoia, recalling Mace's obsession with counter surveillance.

"You laugh now, but you can never be too careful." *He glared at Axe and me as we laughed at him.*

Axe huffed. "I swear you came out of Mom looking over your shoulder."

"Considering you were right behind me, I'd say I had reason to watch my back," Mace shot back at him with a shoulder punch.

Fraternal twins, Mace and Axe shared a tight bond, making me wonder what it would have been like to have a sibling. I shook the memory off; it wasn't good to dwell in the past – my father had taught me that. I threw my bag on the bed and stripped down for a shower. I let the water pour over me, loosening the crusted blood of my victim from my hands and arms. As the warm water revived my spirit I summoned up the memories of the session, trying to find anything I could use outside of the knowledge that the boss was away. I scrubbed my skin in anger at my luck grabbing a runt that was so loyal. With the last of the soap rinsed from my hair and skin, I turned the dial to cold, catching my breath as the icy water hit my flesh, bringing sweet relief from the hot night air.

Throwing on a pair of jeans and a tank, I reset the hair in my doorway and headed down for a bite to eat. The room was empty so I took a seat in the back. Elena didn't keep me waiting long, bouncing in to ask, "Hungry?"

"Very." I smiled. "Bring me anything and I'll devour it."

"I have *menudo rojo* on the stove. I'll grab you a bowl." She disappeared into the kitchen, leaving me to my thoughts.

Images of my captive's screams as I broke his fingers brought a smile to my lips. Normally torture made me ill, but the thought of making them suffer one by one felt good – justified. What we did was horrible, but we did it for the right reasons and in the name of our country and for the greater good. It wasn't really murder, not really. My team had earned the right to pick and choose our jobs, focusing on the most vile criminals and warlords. And while I understood Huron had been compromised, and the action the agency took to protect itself, we had earned more loyalty. No, Mace and Axe didn't deserve what they got, and those that killed them would pay, no matter what. I would see this through.

The hair on the back of my neck stood up. Someone was watching me. Without lifting my eyes, I scanned the room. Sure enough I found the dark-haired man they called Alejandro sitting at the bar not bothering to hide the fact he was staring at me.

I called out to him, "Can I help you with something?"

"I think it is you who is in need of help," he drawled back at me.

"Oh, Don Alejandro, I didn't hear you come in," Elena said, returning with my dinner and placing in front of me. "I made *menudo rojo*, would you care for a bowl?"

He nodded and added, "And fresh tortillas?"

"Of course!" She laughed, returning to the kitchen.

As soon as she was gone, I demanded, "Are you following me?"

"Me?"

I narrowed my eyes and snapped, "Yes, you!" Waving my hand around the room, I asked, "Do you see anyone else here or perhaps you thought I was speaking to myself?" Once again I found myself being rude for no reason at all.

His head shook as he chuckled. "No, I am not following you."

After the adrenalin high of my afternoon his haughty behavior struck a nerve, so I asked, "Then why were you staring at me?"

"I was, what is it you Americans say? 'Taking in the sights.'" He turned his blue eyes upon me, pouring on the charm as he said, "Surely a woman as beautiful as you is used to men admiring you from a far."

Not impressed by his pick-up line, I rolled my eyes. "We call that stalking and it's a crime in America," I said.

A flood of locals streamed through the door, and Elena returned with his bowl, and yet another attempt at matchmaking. "You should join Señora October, she is wonderful company," she said with a smile. Turning her attention to me she added, "It isn't safe for a woman as pretty as you to be here on her own, sit with Don Alejandro and no one will bother you."

"I can protect her from here should anyone bother her, but the lady has made her wish to be left alone perfectly clear," he said as he turned toward his meal.

Elena frowned at me but didn't push, collecting my empty bowl and scolded, "I wish you wouldn't eat so fast, it's not good for you."

"I told you not to cook so well and I wouldn't be forced to eat so quickly." Elena bounced off to help her other guests. I stood, pushing in my chair, meeting the eyes of my protective stranger.

He stared at me and I felt suddenly exposed, as if he were looking into my deepest thoughts. He held my gaze for a brief moment before speaking. "Be back before dark, these hills are not safe after the sun goes down."

"I can take care of myself," I assured him, spinning on my heel, feeling his eyes boring into my back as I headed for my room.

***

The hot night made sleep impossible. My father's discipline lessons were stretched to their limits, but I was able to force my body to rest while my mind bounced between thoughts of how to break my captive and Alejandro's blue eyes. Try as I might, I couldn't keep his face from my thoughts. Five minutes before the alarm would have gone off, I turned it off, quickly dressed, gathered my gear, and headed down to the kitchen. Diego was waiting for me, blocking the door.

He scratched at his head and hesitantly said, "You agreed to be back every night before dark."

"What am I, grounded?"

My joke earned a glare from the usually happy man. He wiggled a finger at me while scowling and said, "Things are different here, and you came alone."

"Diego." I sighed, "I know about the bandits in the hills. I'm being careful and not climbing anywhere near them." I promised aloud as I reached for the door handle behind him.

Frowning down at me he insisted, "Be back before dark or I will come looking for you this time."

Pushing past him I shook my head, not believing the amount of attention I was receiving this trip. My persona called for being a friendly tourist, but this is ridiculous. I would have to ensure I wrapped things up because there was no way I could come back here again. With my brunch bag in hand I left the kitchen, avoiding Diego's eyes as I marched past him out to my Jeep.

My anger drove me back to the villa faster than wisdom dictated was safe, proving my judgment had been affected after losing my team. *I'm losing my temper too often, I have to sort this out or my days are numbered.* Busy talking to myself, I took the steps into the villa two at a time, swinging the door open harder than intended. As the door slammed open my captive's head jerked upright with a hiss.

Blinking back my confusion, I shouted, "What the Hell!" Astonished at the physical changes, I tried to wrap my mind around what I was seeing. His skin was notably paler, and though he still seemed weak, his face and arms held no evidence of the damage I had wrought on his body. His gnarled, broken hand no longer held the dark purple bruises, they were now yellowed and appeared to be days old – mangled but healing. But above all, his eyes stopped me in my tracks. His once prosaic hazel eyes now seemed to glow an unnatural gold as they studied my every move.

As I neared his side he struggled to lift his head higher, demanding, "I need blood."

Peering down at him I was at a complete loss, and asked, "What in the name of hell are you?"

Chortling he beckoned. "Come closer and I'll show you." Bewildered, I wracked my brain trying to figure out what to do. "I will be free eventually, and when I am, I'll use your blood to fully regenerate."

His sinister laughter deepened, going straight to my spine with the challenge in his voice. Turning, I fixed my eyes on him while crossing my arms, and asking, "What are you?"

He smiled, pulling back his lips to reveal a set of long eyeteeth. "Something you'll wish you never met." He scoffed.

I slammed his head back on the chair, dazing him momentarily, then carefully pulled his lips upward for a closer look. "Son of a..." He jerked his head to the side, grazing my skin with his teeth but not breaking the skin. I drove my elbow into his cheek bone, slicing him open once again. Stumbling backward, I couldn't believe this was really happening. "Vampires don't exist," I whispered to myself. I shook my head as he lapped at the blood spilling down his cheek. "This can't be happening."

He glared at me and said, "I told you, you can't kill me." His eyes laughed at my disbelief as he continued, taunting, "My friends will come for me, and you'll be ripped to shreds."

"Everything that bleeds can die," I assured him as I ran my hands over the items on the table, settling on a long dagger. "I've decided I don't need you alive." I drove the dagger deep into his chest, causing him to let out a scream as the blade pierced his heart, but after the initial pain passed, he lifted his head, laughing at the astonishment on my face. Pulling the knife out in bewildered disgust, I shook my head, at a loss for what to do next.

As I took a few steps back he taunted me again. "Don't run away, we're just starting to have some fun."

I waved a hand over my tools as I assured him it wasn't over. "If these won't do the job then I'll find something that does." Carefully, I shoved a rag in his mouth taping it shut and ran for the Jeep. *Vampires! This can't be happening, I must be going crazy.* It happened sometimes when an operative goes solo for too long, first they think the agency wants them dead, then they snap completely going rogue. It's why we are given handlers in the first place, to make sure we are dealing well with the emotional disconnect with society, but how could I deny what I had just seen with my own eyes?

I found myself at the bar before I even realized I had put the Jeep in motion. Diego stared cautiously till he determined it was safe to ask, "Are you ill?"

"No, bring me a Jack and Bailey's," I stammered.

Diego frowned at my choice of rotgut, checked his watch and said, "It's only seven in the morning."

"Make it a double," I whispered as I ran my hands over my face as I let my mind wander.

I've seen evil. The assignments we were given showcased so many forms of evil that I would have thought I was prepared for anything. Why should this rattle me? There was no question in my mind that my team's demise was causing me to take risks and make mistakes. I have seen so much death, and I have felt its sting myself. Have I simply reached my breaking point?

I sat there for several hours alone with my concerns over my own insanity, nursing a never-ending drink, and being stared at by one overly concerned bartender. Once I got over the shock of what I had discovered, I made a mental list of every conceivable death for a vampire reported by Hollywood. If vampires were real then maybe, just maybe, some movie got it right.

A newly-familiar, velvety voice pulled me into the present. "Would you like to talk about whatever has you drowning in whiskey before noon?"

"You wouldn't believe me if I told you," I whispered, taking another swig of my fresh glass. "Don't worry, this is my last one."

My handsome stranger smiled at Diego and said, "I'll have the same as the lady." Diego grimaced but poured Alejandro a drink walking away muttering under his breath. I watched my unwanted drinking companion's face as he took his first drink. Closing his eyes he shook his head involuntary at the drink's potency. With repressed disgust he asked, "You like this stuff?"

"I didn't ask you to join me," I replied.

He sighed. "True. Still you're obviously troubled and I may be able to help."

"No one can help me," I blurted out. "And it wouldn't be worth their effort if they could." Pushing my half-empty glass away I turned to Alejandro, grabbed him by the collar and pulling his lips to mine. I drank in the taste of him, then abruptly let go of the stunned man. "Don't get excited," I said, and lied, "I'm climbing a difficult cliff face today and wanted to recall what that tasted like in case it's the last time I get the chance."

"And?"

I smiled down at him, placing a finger on his lips as I said, "If I make it back, I'll take another after dinner." Spinning on my heel, I made for the stairs, adjusting my pace so I didn't fall over as the alcohol caught up with me.

He called after me, "I'll see you at dinner, but I am picking the drinks."

Slamming my door, I leaned against it with a thump, asking myself, "What am I doing?" I shook my head at my stupidity. "I've lost my mind. Vampires, booze and now I think I asked a guy out on a date. What the hell am I thinking?" I pushed my palm against my forehead over and over. "Pull yourself together, Beau, or you are going to end up dead. And now I'm talking to myself, this is ridiculous." Needing to clear my head, I made for the shower, adjusting the water temperature to lukewarm, letting it beat down on my face till I could think straight once again.

I resolved to attack this like any other challenge; gather intelligence, formulate a plan, and execute. Forget the fact there was a vampire waiting for my return. If life had taught me anything, it's everything dies. Of course I would question my sanity after seeing a vampire. What sane person wouldn't? I still had to act, I couldn't alter my course. My team would be avenged.

I dressed quickly, and ran a comb through my curls before pulling them back into my usual braid. Rejuvenated, I gathered my bag and took one last look in the mirror. "You can do this, they have to die!" Something in the mirror caught my attention; slowly I turned toward my bed with a half-smile. "Why not?" I pulled the wooden cross off the wall and shoved it in my bag. A quick stop in the kitchen produced garlic for good measure then I headed outside.

I tossed my bag in the Jeep as Diego stepped out on the porch, inquiring, "Are you feeling better?"

"I am, thank you." I smiled at him. "Sorry for the drama." I didn't wait for his reply, firing up the Jeep and heading deeper into town to my next destination. Pulling up to the large white church I hesitated, the last time I stepped foot in a church was when I buried my father. A knot formed in my stomach with the memory, it was also the last day I ever heard anyone refer to me by my real name. Grabbing an empty bottle I squared my shoulders and walked in with purpose, straight to the stoup.

A soft voice called to me, "Have you come for confession, my child?"

Turning slowly I bent my head toward the priest smiling up at me and said, "Not today, Father, I just need some Holy water."

"For what purpose?" he asked.

Uncomfortable lying to a priest yet unwilling to admit the truth, I searched for middle ground. Tilting my head to the side I admitted, "Protection."

His face grew serious as he reached for my bottle. "Allow me," he said as he sprinkled water from the stoup over my bottle three times. "This bottle is blessed by the sprinkling of this Holy water, in the name of the Father, and of the Son, and of the Holy Spirit," he proclaimed. Dipping the bottle into the stoup he let it fill to the top then sprinkled something from a pouch at his waist into the bottle while whispering something in Latin. Seemingly finished he turned his eyes upon me and asked, "When was your last confession?"

"Prior to my father's death," I admitted. "Father, I am beyond saving. I tread a fine line between heaven and hell, but I trust my actions make the world safer for others."

Squinting up at me as if examining my inner being, he slowly handed me the bottle and said, "This will ward off evil. Go with God, my child, and know that no one is beyond His forgiveness. He protects those that protect others, and when you are done with your business, come back to see me for confession." He raised his hand making the sign of the cross while saying a blessing.

I fled the church more affected by his words than I cared to admit. As I rounded the bend out of town, I slowed the Jeep to a stop. Searching the brush, I found two suitable heavy sticks tossing them in my bag, completing my makeshift vampire torture kit.

A few minutes later I pushed the door open to find my captive waiting for me with a smile on his lips. "I was hoping you were foolish enough to come back," he said, "now I won't have to go far to get dinner."

Pulling up a rickety chair I swung my leg over it and sat down, dropping the bag at my feet. I steadied my nerves and asked, "Are you that eager to die?" Retrieving a stick I pulled a knife from my boot and began to whittle the end into a sharp point.

"You still think you are going to kill me, don't you?" he asked.

Without looking up from my work I let my peripheral vision examine his restraints, another hour or so and he would be free. Sloppy yet again, my actions were almost begging me to fail. Disappointed with my laziness, I examined my options. I could rebind him, or get this over with and have less to untie when I disposed of his body. His gloating boasts that I couldn't kill him gave me pause but I had yet to discover my match. Pushing down the fear that was rising to the surface, I glanced up at him lazily. "I know I am going to kill you. What we're going to explore together is how, exactly I am going to make that happen."

He threw back his head with a hearty laugh. "This isn't some movie and you aren't some slayer. All you are is dinner!"

Finishing with my two stakes, I pulled out the garlic and started peeling the cloves. "Speaking of dinner."

His laughter grew as he choked out, "Garlic? Are you really going to try to kill me with garlic?"

"I'm not counting anything out," I answered without looking up. Satisfied with the amount of raw garlic in my hand I moved to the back of his chair. "If garlic isn't a problem then you have nothing to fear do you? Open your mouth and let's see."

"Open my mouth yourself, bitch." He taunted.

I took a deep breath, letting it out with a sigh. "You need new material, but if you insist." Slamming my hand into his hyoid, his mouth automatically opened, allowing me to shove the garlic down his throat while he gasped for air. "It seems you still require oxygen." Tilting his head backward I poured Holy water directly into his heaving mouth then held his mouth shut, forcing his oxygen-starved throat to swallow.

Backing away I watched as he struggled to regain precious air, his arms straining against the tape, loosening the restraints further in his rage. His eyes latched onto me full of hatred, but all he could do was scream. Oddly fascinated, I couldn't tear my eyes away as he writhed in pain. Finally he screamed at me, "Holy water! You fucking bitch!" He tore his arms free, flailing in pain but determined to fight back.

As he ripped the ropes off his arms and legs I doused him with the rest of the Holy water, it bore into him like acid, eliciting another round of hair-raising screams. Quickly I drove a wooden stake into his chest, piercing his heart. His head sank to his chest in defeat allowing me to take a deep breath of relief. I moved in to check for a pulse.

His hand clutched my wrist in a vice-worthy grip.

A slow, sickening laugh rolled from my victim, growing louder as he raised his head to stare at me and growl, "I told you; you can't kill me."

I couldn't believe what I was seeing; my disbelief momentarily immobilized me. "It can't be true." I shook my head as he stood up, completely free. I whispered, "That should have killed you."

"Why?" He laughed. "Because some writer said it would? It has to be blessed silver, dumb little girl. Do you happen to have any?" He said with a snarl. "It's your turn for some pain." He smiled at me with raw, holy-water burnt lips. I reached for my bag just as he slammed a hand into my face, sending me and my things flying through the air. He roared as he stretched his stiff body. "This is going to feel good." Pulling the stake from his chest he turned toward me and barked, "I wonder if you'll like this shoved this into your chest."

Scrambling backward, my hand caught my bag. I reached in pulling out the last item – the cross. Shoving it out in front of me, I said, "Stay away from me."

His laughter sent chills up my spine. "That might work if you were a priest." He chortled. Looming over me he swatted the cross out of my hand then a kick sent me skidding into the wall. He continued to laugh as he asked, "Where are you going?" Slowly he walked toward me, savoring his regained freedom. "I can't decide if I want to turn you into a Creeper, watch them tear you apart, or simply drain you dry."

I watched as my death came closer with his every step. I didn't tremble with fear, I always knew I would be killed in combat, but if I was going to die I'd go out fighting. I slid my hands into my boots pulling out my brass knuckles and stood to meet him face to face.

He smiled at my audacity and sneered. "You have a snowball's chance in hell."

I raised my hands as I prepared to meet death head on. "My dad didn't raise me to back away from a fight, you'll have to work to kill me," I said with as much pride as I could summon.

In a blur his hand moved, it was suddenly wrapped around my throat, lifting me up against the wall. He smiled once more as he gloated over his coming victory. "Had we met under different circumstances I may have asked my master if I could keep you as a pet."

Automatically my hand went to his, trying to pull his grip from my throat. He squeezed harder, closing off my air supply. I brought my other hand down on his temple, driving my knuckle in as deep as I could over and over. Pulling me back to his chest, he slammed me into the wall, catching my shoulder blade on the windowsill and knocking the wind out of me. Frantic, I tried to find leverage against the window fame to relieve the weight of my body and stop from choking. I pulled wildly at the mattress covering the window, feeling the rotting material pulling free and offering no leverage.

His grip loosened and he began screaming. Pushing myself against the wall, I brought my feet up driving them into his chest and pushing him away from me. Realizing he was screaming as his skin sizzled in the light pouring in from the window, I tore the rest of the mattress down. "I bet that's a bitch," I called to him as he dropped to his knees, glaring up at me in pain as the sun inflicted punishment I could have never delivered. Bits of his flesh turned to ash, peeling off and drifting into the air around me. I drove my heel into his black-charred face, staring as he disintegrated into a pile of ash. Stunned, I sank to my knees, compelled to gawk at all that remained of my murderess captive.

CHAPTER ⬥————— FOUR

Still dazed, I sat down at a table in the back of the cantina trying to come to terms with the impossible. Muffled voices buzzed in my head, a hand waved in my face rocked me from my thoughts. I looked up into a set of beautiful blue eyes waiting for a response. Shaking my free of the shock I asked, "I'm sorry, what?"

"I was saying you're early," Alejandro said, frowning down at me. "Are you well?"

I tossed my head back, pulling out my braid, hoping to hide behind the masses of my red curls before I answered, "I'm fine, thank you."

"You're hurt," he said as his hand jutted toward my neck. Instinctively I blocked his move but he caught my hand in his, surprising me with his quickness. He whispered, "Let me see." His fingertips were as gentle as his voice, making it impossible to say no. My stomach fluttered at his touch. I pulled back trying hide the reaction he was having on me – I didn't want him to feel the change in my heart rate. But it was no use. His fingers reached for me again, tracing the red welts on my neck. His back went stiff and he demanded, "Who did this to you?"

"I fell during my climb," I lied, "it's nothing."

Sliding his palm over the welts to gage the size, he pushed for more information. "These welts are from a man's hand. Tell me who did this!" An odd chirp drew his attention to the end of the bar saving me further explanation. I followed the sound and saw a man's figure move within the shadows. Alejandro tilted his head toward me and said, "Excuse me a moment."

The figure seemed able to stay within the shadows, not comfortable being seen. Alejandro leaned in, the two exchanging conversation. A leather clad finger extended from the shadows pointing in my direction, and Alejandro turned staring at me in shock. As fast as the figure had appeared he melted into the darkness, leaving me to speculate if it was this person that had been following me since my arrival.

Alejandro picked up a bottle of wine and two glasses from the bar then took the seat next to me, his face bearing a mixture of surprise and disapproval. He whispered, "It seems you're full of surprises." He didn't bother to hide his disappointment. "It seems we need to talk about your recent actions."

Glaring at him, I demanded, "Have you had someone tailing me?"

He shrugged. Opening the bottle, he simply said, "I make it my business to know what is happening in town."

"You knew!" My anger pushed me to my feet as understanding swept through me. I threw my arm out, pointing toward the door. "You knew they were out there!"

Alejandro smiled at the people sitting a few tables over who were now staring at my outburst and whispered, "Please sit down and try not to make a scene."

Fuming, yet strangely relieved that I was not alone in the knowledge that vampires were real, I sat, taking the glass of wine he offered. I stared back at the couple now whispering, and asked, "Can I help you with something, or would you like me to come over and listen to your conversation?" They turned away, irritated at being called out for their busybody behavior.

My companion chuckled. "Settle down, now."

Leaning in on my elbows I pressed my forehead into my hands, shaking my head back and forth. "I just can't believe it," I said under my breath. "I've seen a lot of evil in this world, but I would have never believed this if I hadn't just lived it."

Alejandro let out a sigh. "I can't believe you're alive. What were you thinking?"

"I needed answers." I dropped my hands and whispered, "I didn't set out to prove the existence of vampires." I took a sip from the glass he offered. "This is very good, I don't normally drink wine, and when I do, I prefer white," I said.

He smiled at my compliment and said, "It's from Spain, my mother's family to be specific." Staring at his glass as if looking at treasure, he continued, "There are only twelve bottles remaining of this particular year."

"It's delicious." Staring at him I added, "I thought you might be a Spaniard, I'm out of practice with my dialects but if I had to guess I would say Basque – and then there are those blue eyes."

He inclined his head. "You would be correct." He smirked. "Blue eyes and all." Tapping the bottle he added, "As for the wine, I am honored you like it." He sat back in his chair his eyes lingering on my bruises. He took and another long sip, and said, "He could have easily broken your neck."

My hand went to my neck, covering the evidence of my altercation, and whispered, "I'm fine. I've had worse."

His brows came together with his question, "What do you do for a living that you have had worse beatings? Are you a police officer?"

"Military brat," I admitted.

He shook his head, and said, "I am sorry, this is not a term I am aware of."

"My father was a Navy SEAL and I grew up on various bases." I smiled at his blank stare and continued, "Americans refer to kids like me as 'military brats'."

Still confused, he inquired, "And you beat each other up?"

"Sometimes." I laughed. "When you are raised by SEALs with hand-to-hand combat training, you're given an early education, so if you are put in a situation where you need to defend yourself, it's second nature."

He shook his head at me and said, "I am not sure I would want my little girl, if I had one, to beat up all the boys at school."

"I'm glad my father didn't think like that." I scoffed. "None of the boys messed with me after I broke Tommy Swanson's arm when he went for second base." Alejandro's face went blank, making me laugh harder. "He tried to put his hand up my shirt," I explained.

Alejandro put his glass to his lips and mumbled, "For a moment I felt sorry for the little guy." He took a sip then winked at me, affirming, "We are agreed. All my girls shall know how to defend against little Tommy Swanson's unwanted advancements." He grew serious. "But where I come from, your brothers would have ensured your safety, and you would have been free to grow up like a lady without fear of unwanted suitors."

"No brothers or sisters," I said with a quick shake of my head. "My mother died shortly after I was born." Suddenly I realized I was having a real conversation and sharing truths I had long ago buried.

He sensed my mood change and countered, "I'm sorry. Do you have any family left?"

"No, I am the last of my clan." Wanting to shift the conversation back to him I asked, "You?"

"My father and sister are gone, as are my two uncles." He frowned down at his empty glass clearly struggling with sharing his own past. "My mother isn't well and is...away." He took a deep breath before he added, "And my brother has a disgraceful habit."

When he didn't go on I asked, "Drugs or alcohol?"

A grimace etched its way to the corners of his mouth. "I guess you could call it a drug. As it stands he is not welcome in my home until he stops what he is doing," he said remorsefully. "Until he regains control, if he can, and my mother's pain lessens, I am like you. Alone."

"You are nothing like me," I whispered, turning my head to stare into my glass. "I am a bird of passage. I have no home, no family, no name, no....hope." Lifting my head I stared into the blue pools of his eyes and said, "You have a chance that your family will come back to you, don't give that up. Do whatever you need to keep your family safe."

He ran his fingertips along the line of my jaw, sending shivers down my spine. "I wish I could share with you how wrong and how right you are, but some secrets are better left untold." He stood, pulling my hand up with him, and asked, "Would you dance with me?"

"I don't dance; I'm afraid I never learned how," I admitted.

His smile drew me to my feet as his lips brushed the top of my hand. "Dance with me," he said as he pulled me into his arms. I heard the music grow louder. Until this moment it had just been soft background noise. Pulling me close, he whispered, "Feel the music tell you what to do, let me be your guide."

My heart pounded out a warning. I couldn't breathe; my mind spun in delight, and my body betrayed me with its desire to pull him closer. An unfamiliar feeling engulfed me, one I had not experienced since I was a child. I felt safe. The way I felt when my father came home on leave and first took me in his arms - safe and secure with the knowledge that nothing could harm me while I was tucked in his arms – that no one would dare hurt me.

I pulled back enough to look in his eyes, fascinated as they shifted to a lighter shade of blue and I knew he was just as hungry for me as I was for him. He pulled back the hair from my neck, brushing his lips against the tattoo behind my ear. "This is lovely," he whispered.

My skin hummed at the touch of his lips and I thought I might pass out from the pleasure. "It is a reminder," I offered.

Pushing my mane back further, he spotted more of the branch. "How far down your body does this go?" he asked. I opened my mouth to answer, and he cut me off, whispering, "No don't tell me, it will only make me want you more." He claimed my lips, sending my mind reeling. He pulled my body into the curve of his, allowing me to feel every muscle flex as he groaned in pleasure. Alejandro tried to pull away, but my mouth would not allow him to go, my lips followed his as they retreated until he gave in, driving his lips into mine again.

The passion between us threatened my sanity. Slowly he pulled away, resting his lips just above my ear and whispered a reminder. "We are in public." His erratic breaths proof that his body felt the same as mine.

"I'm sorry," I whispered, "I've never wanted anyone so badly in my life."

"Nor have I," he said with a hard swallow. "But I am keeping you from dinner and if you stay in my arms I am afraid I won't ever let you go."

He took a step back, and I resisted pulling him back into my arms. Instead I focused on keeping the room from spinning as he walked us back to the table. I sat down in the chair he pulled out, and listened as he ordered our meal, all, the while trying to understand what was happening to my body and why I was no longer in control of it. My heart screaming at me that I was falling in love, while my mind shouted that this was a trap. My body begged me to give into my desire for this dark-haired stranger with the beautiful blue eyes and lips that tasted like honey.

We ate in silence, neither able to put our feelings into words. The dining room filled up, then emptied, and still we sat staring at each other, barely breathing, let alone uttering a sound. A chirp sounded at the end of the bar; his shadowy companion had returned. Reluctantly he stood and said, "Give me a moment."

I watched as the black-clad figure leaned toward Alejandro, giving his report within the darkness that seemed to move at his will. With a nod, Alejandro returned to the table, stretching his hands toward mine with an apology. "I am sorry but something has come up that demands my attention."

Taking his hand, I allowed him to pull me to my feet. I said, "I understand."

He bent forward, intent on kissing my lips. Then, hesitating for a moment, he smiled, changing his mind and brushing his lips over my hand instead. Bent over my hand, he smiled up at me and said, "Until next we meet."

Like a blur he was out the door, leaving me to the knowing smile of Elena at the bar. She winked at me but said nothing. I ran my hands over my face, trying to clear my head as I made my way up the stairs for bed. I barely remembered to check the hair in the door. Finding it untouched, I pushed the door open and threw myself down on the bed.

My mind raced over the events of the night, recalling each touch of his lips on my skin, each brush of his fingertips, and above all else the hunger in his eyes. No man had ever had this effect on me. Love was a weakness. This was something I had told myself over and over in my teenage years. As I grew older, I followed my father's example, simply taking care of the desire with the act of sex. I sat up at the thought and said to myself, "That's what I need to do. Just have sex with him and that'll be the end of this schoolgirl fantasy."

Kicking my boots off, I pulled the covers over me, not bothering to undress, allowing myself the luxury of the memories of being in his arms while surrounded by the smell of him on my clothes. As I recalled each moment I started to doubt my theory. *What if sex makes you want him more? What if this is love?* No, desire is soon quenched – it might take a few times, but passion doesn't last. As for love, it muddies up life. And when it leaves you, it leaves an emptiness you can never fill. It's better not to love, better to leave yourself without weaknesses others can exploit.

I closed my eyes, willing my body to rest amid the various memories of my dark knight, Alejandro. As before, his eyes haunted my dreams, but this time they were alive with hunger, a hunger I wanted to consume me.

The morning sun smiled down upon me, rousing me from my slumber. I sat up, stretching my sore body. Spying the clock on my nightstand, I jumped from the bed in a hurry. I had far too much to do today to allow myself to sleep in. And yet that was exactly what I had done. I couldn't recall the last time I had slept beyond seven in the morning. I huffed, disgusted at myself for forgetting to set the alarm then recalled why. Staring into the mirror I brushed the white petals tattooed on the side of my neck, reliving the touch of his lips upon my skin.

Shaking my head I spoke firmly to the woman in the mirror, "Pull it together, Beau. Today we get what we came here for." I pointed at my image and said sharply, "No school girl fantasies today."

I ran a comb through my wild mane, then braided it tight, brushed my teeth, changed clothes then quickly readied my room, and went down for breakfast. Elena was busy this morning so I was thankfully spared her matchmaking and was able to eat in peace, and plan the day.

Since torture provided no intel on the compound, I was left with frontal assault. Today I would employ a hit-and-run tactic. My captive had proven even the scrawny ones were stronger than I was, so I needed to avoid my preferred hand-to-hand combat. I would fall back on my ability to be calculating. I would find a way to get them into the sun and watch them burn to nothingness.

Pulling up in front of their compound, I checked my watch, 0900. I frowned down at my late start, but unable to turn back the hands of time, I jumped out of the Jeep. I rifled through my weapons in the back till I drug out Axe's crossbow. Further digging revealed the last remaining box of tranquilizers. Maybe this would do the trick, I thought as I repacked the gear I had dislodged. I recalled the runt knocking the wind out of me when he hit me. Setting the crossbow down, I dug deeper till I found the bag that held my body armor.

A few minutes later I was dressed in a full set of Kevlar body armor, three crossbow bolts coated with tranquilizer in hand. As prepared as I could be, I whispered under my breath, "Ready or not boys, here comes trouble!" I stayed in the shadows of the buildings as much as possible, not allowing myself to forget the image of Axe going down from the bullet to the eye. They may be vampires, but they weren't afraid to use a gun.

I advanced carefully, not allowing myself to rely on the knowledge the camp was never active before dusk; I had to be ready for anything. I reached the first door, looking around prior to testing the knob. It was unlocked. *Let's add arrogance to the list of their weaknesses, maybe it will give me an advantage.* I opened the door slowly, leaving it ajar a full minute while listening for footsteps before I inched my way in, staying crouched with my back to the wall.

I was just about to move forward when I heard something above me. I quickly turned my eyes and crossbow toward the sound. A man hung from a rafter ten feet above me, further examination left me with more questions than I had answers. He seemed to be hanging by his knees with his eyes shut and he wasn't bound in any visible way. I shook my head, asking myself, "*Who would voluntarily hang upside down?*" I stifled down a laugh when an image of a bat popped into my head. *Maybe they really think they're bats.* Hugging the wall, I made a round trying to ascertain if it would be possible to take the bat lover from the rafters without drawing more down upon me.

The room was clear, so I returned to the doorway to set up for my first victim. This would be a good gage of what was to come, and he was close enough to the door for a quick run to sunlight. He was bigger than the runt I first took. I anticipated a larger fight from this one, and hoped no one heard.

I lined up for a head shot since capture wasn't my goal, if he died before I got him outside it wouldn't hurt my feelings at all. I let lose the bolt as I exhaled, and watched it strike him right between the eyes. As he fell toward the floor I rushed him, trying to pull him out of the building before he awakened. He stirred just as I hit the doorframe. I pulled with all my might on his large lanky frame, getting him half way through the doorway before he realized what was happening.

Snarling at me he flipped over to his stomach, holding onto one side of the doorframe refusing to be drug out into the sun. Thankfully he was still groggy, but he was definitely stronger than my runt. His eyes rolled back in his head as he dug his nails into the wooden frame. He hissed, "What the hell do you think you're doing?"

"Inviting you to a barbeque." I grunted as I pulled again. He didn't budge, reaching with one hand to pull out the arrow while hanging onto the doorway with the other. Seeing the opportunity, I slammed my boot into his hand that was holding the door, and gave a yank as I felt him let go. He snarled at the ground I gained and dug his nails into the wood of the porch, leaving the arrow lodged in his forehead. We were locked in battle, me pulling him toward the light and him digging into the wood to stay in the shadow of the porch. Shoving my knee into his back I let go of his feet and pushed the front of his head into the porch.

He screamed in pain as the bolt took its journey deeper, flailing about, allowing me to drag him to the steps. Turning over on his back, he finally got smart, kicking at me with his feet. "Come to momma, big boy, death awaits you." I watched the rhythm of his feet, timing my counterattack with perfection. On his next big thrust I pulled in conjunction with his momentum, flipping him forward as I rolled toward his head, propelling him into the sunlit air. He fried before my eyes, his ashes scattering in the wind. I scrambled to the Jeep, surveying the area to see if anyone had come to his aid.

My body spent, I gazed down at my watch and sighed, nearly noon. This is taking too long. I need a faster regress with less physical interaction. I returned to the gear in the Jeep, searching for an answer to my problem. Buried at the bottom of the canvas bag I found a possible solution. Pulling my hand out I smiled down at Axe's spear gun, his words coming back to mind from the day he brought it home. *He shrugged at our laughter, "You never know when we might need this."*

I smiled, thankful for Axe's need for all things of the killing variety. I tapped the shaft in my hand. "You'll never know how right you were, you big, wonderful weapon hoarder." I set the spear gun down on the hood circling back to grab the box of tranquilizers and slamming my knee into the winch on the front of the Jeep. I sucked in my scream of pain, not wanting to draw any unwanted attention. Instead I expressed my anger staring down at the winch and silently cussing it out, till a memory smacked me in the face. "It might work," I said to myself, dashing for the key chain in the ignition, which doubled as the remote for the winch. I ran back to the winch patting it like a loyal dog.

A few minutes later I had the cable from the winch attached to the end of the spear, the remote in my pocket, and was ready to hunt. I laughed at the memory of a vampire movie I had once watched and the crazy notion the Jeep had my flank. "Hollywood, me, and my four-wheeled back-up. What a team." I took a deep breath to steady myself and said, "Let's try this."

My new system worked well, I pulled them out one by one. Each put up a different fight, some digging at the floor, others furniture, and the smarter ones hanging onto the doorjambs till I hacked their fingers free. I let the Jeep do the pulling, freeing me to simply clear the way to the porch. I did manage to bag one head before the sunlight took it, intent on sending it back to Conrad as evidence when I filed my report. I would acid off the flesh and send back the clean skull as proof I wasn't crazy, I simply had to ensure the skull didn't see sunlight. Sunlight, what a lovely idea! On my next ingress I took my time, leaving behind some hidden surprises for my next visit.

After my seventh vampire turned to dust, I contemplated going for one more, but darkness was nearing and although I had yet to find more than one in each room I had to venture deeper and deeper into their hold for my prey. Either way, I had reached the end of the winch's cable. Deciding to err on the side of caution, I packed up, allowing myself to feel the anticipation of possibly seeing Alejandro at dinner.

My only regret of the day was not knowing what impact killing these seven had on their numbers. After checking my security hair, I entered my room, took a quick shower, then set up my acid wash for the skull in the sink, pulling the head from the bag my lips curled up at the smell. "You stink worse than Axe's gas, and that's saying something," I said to the lifeless head. Careful not to splash the acid on my skin, I slid the head into the solution and went down for dinner.

I waited at the back table, feeling like a teenager on her first date, my eyes rarely leaving the doorway. Odd as it may seem, I felt him enter before I saw him, watching as he made his way to me without taking his eyes off mine. He took my hand, pulling it to his lips as he said, "You have no idea how much I missed your company today."

"Flattery may get you more than you ask for," I teased.

A brow arched at me as he asked, "Does that mean your heart missed my presence as well?"

I hesitated but decided to be honest, and said, "It did indeed." I ran a finger over his lips. "But not as much as my lips missed yours."

His eyes flashed with desire as he motioned toward the seat next to me and inquired, "May I join you?"

"I wouldn't allow another to take your seat," I replied, earning another white smile. He went over to the bar to order our dinner then took the seat next to me. Winding a loose red curl around his finger he asked, "Would you trust me with your given name?"

I blinked back my surprise and stammered, "Why do you think my name isn't October?"

He pulled out the band that held my braid, running his fingers through my hair freeing my fire-red mane then whispered, "You told me as much last night." He paused while I mentally replayed our conversation, searching for my lapse. With a sigh he refreshed my memory. "You said you had no name, which implies that the one you are using is false." He traced the white petals of my tattoo and my skin hummed at his touch. Leaning closer he whispered, "I would settle for your true first name, you can withhold your family name till I have earned more of your trust."

"Well, aren't you the clever one?" I asked.

"I pay attention to many things," he said with a shrug. "You seem to be one I watch very closely."

I traced the back of his hand as I informed him, "Knowing me, the real me is...dangerous. I would like to keep you safe."

He smiled widely as he replied, "I could say the same; in fact the strong feelings I'm having for you may have already placed you at risk." He leaned in, kissing me deeply then pulled back slightly to speak, his lips brushed mine as he admitted, "I am sorry if I have endangered you, but I find you irresistible. My heart has never stirred until now. I know it would be wisest to hold my emotions inside, to let you pass by and live your life as intended, but God forgive me - I cannot."

Though it bordered on insanity I allowed his words to take root in my heart. My walls were falling as I kissed my way up his jawline to his ear then whispered, "Beau. My real name is Beau."

"Thank you for trusting in me, I will not betray that trust," he said while staring intently into my eyes.

I felt his heart racing as I pressed my lips against his pulsing jugular, startled by how fast it was beating, how it matched my own. "I have never known a man that I wanted to share the real me with, until now." Staring into his blue eyes I took a chance, barely believing the words that were forming in my mind and the consequences they could bear on my life. I took a leap and offered him a truth. "Alejandro, everyone I have ever loved has died violently. My life is dangerous; I am hunted by those that I have served, and by families of those I have...killed."

"I too have killed for my country. There is no shame in doing what is required to keep the innocent safe," he said as he lifted my chin.

I searched his eyes but found no judgement or fear. My hand went to the white petals behind my ear that often drew his attention. Covering them I said, "I have taken an innocent life."

Recognition registered in his eyes and he said with a sigh, "I see, you have marked your body with the lives you have taken." He pushed my hand aside lightly, touching the white petals and asked, "Does this one represent the innocent?"

"Yes," I whispered.

He closed his eyes, lowering his voice, "My sins, and the sins of my family run far deeper and yet I still strive to serve good, to do what is right in the eyes of God."

Elena appeared with our dinner and we reluctantly pulled apart so we could eat. I don't recall ever eating a meal so slowly, but his eyes bore into me with each bite, making me savor each morsel. Elena approved of the change, smiling as she took away our dishes.

A glimmer caught my eye and I turned to locate the source finding nothing out of the ordinary, but something had upset Alejandro and I followed his gaze to a stranger standing at the bar. In a blink Alejandro was at his side, I couldn't fathom how fast he had reacted – my senses must be dull due to this newfound desire. I was close enough that if I strained I could make out their words, but to be sure I quietly stood and made my way to Alejandro's back just in time to hear him ask, "Why are you in town?" With the appearance of the stranger, the room emptied in less than a minute, not even Diego or Elena remained.

The tall blond replied respectfully, "There has been an incident that I have been forced to investigate."

Alejandro demanded an answer, "You are aware of the agreement that none of you are to come into town unscheduled, are you not?"

The blond was clearly torn but didn't back down when he answered. "Yes I am. However, when my

Lord returns he will demand answers from me that I will not have unless I investigate the matter."

Alejandro was unmoved by his plight and said, "Then you should have sent word for assistance or waited until he returned rather than risk breaking the treaty."

His respect faded quickly when he caught sight of me and said, "I followed the scent of the intruder and it has lead back to a woman with your scent all over her." He sneered. "So who has broken the treaty?"

Alejandro turned, following his eyes to me then said, "She did not know what she stumbled upon, and has since done no harm."

"No harm?" The blond laughed heartily. "Is that what she has told you?"

I stepped forward, glaring at the blond and asked loudly, "Are you one of them?"

Revealing a healthy set of fangs the blond needled. "One of whom?"

"You murderous pig!" I snarled as I pulled my brass knuckles from my boots. "I will kill every last one of you!"

Alejandro stepped between us, staring at me intently and said, "You do not know what you are saying." He swung a finger back at the blond with another warning. "Uri, go back to the compound and do not come back to town."

Uri raised a finger at me venomously, stating, "She killed eight of my men, that won't go unpunished."

I pushed forward, my anger demanding justice, but Alejandro caught my arm firmly. His grip didn't allow me to close the distance to Uri's side. "I'll show you punishment," I yelled. "Your group killed my entire team. Good men who didn't deserve to die. We are far from even, and I am far from done with the likes of you! You'll wish I never found out you exist." His smile widened, pushing my patience to its breaking point. I lunged forward only to be stopped by Alejandro's firm grip.

Letting out a sigh Alejandro interjected once again. "Uri, get out of town or I will take this as a blatant infringement on the treaty." He waited for the blond to leave then turned his attention on me and said, "I am asking you to think of the people who live here. Think beyond your own pain. Once you go home these people will still need to co-exist here, and until now the treaty has held."

I glared at him, trying to piece together everything I had heard then asked, "How could you broker a treaty with these monsters?"

He closed his eyes and responded with his own question, "Did you really go there today and kill seven more of his men?"

"They are not men." I spat. "They ceased to be that the moment they turned into these things, or perhaps you missed his fangs?"

Grabbing my shoulders, he shook me, asking, "Can't you see how easily they can kill you? There are too many of them for me to protect you; to protect the town."

"We won't need to worry about that if I kill them all!"

He rolled his eyes in frustration and growled. "Do you ever give up?"

"No, I won't give up until I'm dead or they are," I assured him. "I have to do what's right, they have to die. Why can't you see that they must be stopped?"

Throwing his hands in the air he asked, "And after they kill you, or worse turn you into one of them. What will stop them from killing every last man, woman, and child that call this village home?"

I folded my arms across my chest in defiance, answering, "I won't fail. I will kill them all and the town will no longer have to worry."

"You are an arrogant, willful child that has no idea what evil really is," he said as he glared in my direction. "There are hundreds of them, Beau, hundreds. You cannot kill them all before they overwhelm you, and yet your defiance might kill every other innocent here. Would you really risk that for your own personal vengeance?"

Despite my best effort to contain my emotions tears ran down my face. "You paint a very selfish picture of me, but I think you have lost sight of the truth," I whispered. "They have to be stopped - I know it within the depths of my soul." I shook my head, pleading my case. "No one builds an army just to play nice. They were created for a reason, Alejandro. Have you asked yourself why? Maybe you should have before you ran out and made a treaty with their leader."

I started up the stairs with Alejandro's voice following after me. "Please do not go back."

"I am not making any deals with a man that protects blood-thirsty killers," I said as I ran up the stairs. After locking my door I threw myself down on the bed allowing tears to take over for the first time since my father died. I felt shame over my weakness, permitting myself to be absorbed in defeat was unlike me, but I couldn't stop the tears. If my father were here he'd tell me to use my hurt, turn it into resolve - let it fuel my drive to succeed. But he wasn't here and all I could do was weep, disgusted by my childlike weakness.

The morning light brought no new revelation. After cleaning my trophy, I tossed it in a box for Elena to send out then fired up my laptop and sent off a secure e-mail detailing what was on its way and the need to open the box in a room without sunlight. I stumbled down to the kitchen not caring that I had slept in the same outfit I was now wearing. Elena took one look at me and rethought what she was going to say. Her brows furrowed together as she asked, "Did you and Don Alejandro have a fight?"

I answered half-heartedly, "I wouldn't call it a fight. Why?" Her lips pursed together, telling me she was unsure if she should say more. I handed her the box and said, "I need this to go out today." She nodded but it was clear she had more on her mind. "Just say it, Elena!"

She grimaced as she said, "It's just that he spent the night sitting outside your door. He didn't leave until the sun came up. Please forgive me for asking, but have you done something...foolish?"

"I guess it depends on if doing the right thing is classified as foolish these days," I said, rolling my eyes.

Elena took my hand patting it gently, the kind gesture made me uncomfortable to say the least. "Things are different here *pequeña;* the hills hold many threats. Don Alejandro and his family do what they can to keep us safe. If he has advised you, then you should listen."

Pulling my hand back I let out a sigh. "I understand he thinks it's best to leave the vamp-"

"Do not speak of them out loud," she cut me off signing the cross in front of her and rapidly saying a blessing in Spanish. When she was done she pointed a finger at me demanding, "You do what Don Alejandro says or you go home." Turning on her heel she rushed out of the room.

I slumped against the wall, unsure of my next move. Every fiber in my body begged me to go straight to the compound and continue eradicating the vermin, to finish my mission. It would be just, it would be right. But the thought that after I left the innocents in town would be punished once the leader returned made me sick. I wouldn't be able to live with myself if I caused the death of an entire town.

No closer to a decision I started out for the Jeep. What if I kill off the ones that are here now and then booby-trap their own bunker awaiting the leader's return; I could rig the whole hillside to blow. On the other hand, what if I go back and am killed before I empty out the stragglers, would they still take it out on the town? There was no chance of rallying the town to go in as a unit; they were far too afraid. I jammed the gear in first and took off; the bottom line was I needed more intel before I could make a decision.

As I near my destination I made a bold decision and pulled off the road long enough to suit up in my body armor. I slid every concealable weapon into all my nooks and crannies, slung my gun over my back, and fastened a white flag to the end of my spear gun. Once I was fully geared I walked right through their front gate, fairly sure I was either crazy or would soon be reunited with my father.

I called out, "I am here to talk to Uri." When no one answered I fired off a single shot and repeated my demand, "I want to talk to Uri." Every five minutes I fired off a round and demanded to talk with the blond from the night before.

Finally a low rolling laughter poured from the open doorway. "What would possess you to walk into our camp with a white flag?"

Immediately I recognized the deep voice from the night before, and answered, "I want to talk to you."

"You are welcome to come in." He chortled at me.

I shook my head and said, "I'll stay in the sunlight if you don't mind."

"Please forgive me if I don't join you." He scoffed. "Have you come here to apologize for killing my men?"

"I am not apologizing for doing what's right." I sneered. "I came to say that I killed your men, and that the town had nothing to do with it. Come out on the porch where I can see you, so we can talk."

He walked through the door, leaning up against the jam in full view. "Your turn, come to the edge of the sunlight," he prompted.

"I don't think so." I laughed. "You took what three steps? I'll match your effort, but no more."

"What makes you think I won't have you shot where you stand?" he inquired.

Pulling a remote detonator from my pocket I flipped the switch and watched as he looked down at his feet following the sound of the C-4 arming – my gift from the night before. "As long as you play nice I won't blow your ass up."

His white teeth sparkled in the shadow of the porch. "Resourceful and beautiful, but not that smart are you?" he asked. "You have to know by now that we can move quicker than you."

I hit another button triggering five more bundles within his lair, delightfully watching him follow the sounds, signaling his pending sunlit doom. I smiled wide and said, "I'd say I have a fair IQ, high enough to blow out the front of your entire compound before you can get far enough to avoid turning to ash. Oh, and I wouldn't have your little cronies try to disarm them." I wrinkled up my nose at him. "They're wired to blow if tampered with."

"Well played," he said, clearly impressed. "What can I do for you?"

I took another step forward leaning against an outcropping building and said, "I want it clear that this is between us, all of you and little old me. The town has nothing to do with my actions against you, I'm sure they are content to continue with whatever arrangement you've made with them."

"Why are you here?" he asked.

Shaking my head, I scoffed, "Now who has the lesser IQ? I told you last night, you and your little minions killed off my team."

He laughed. "And now we have to pay?"

Pushing my body off the wall I glared at him and said, "Someone does."

"If you try to kill more of us, you will die," he insisted. Crossed his arms, he added, "No amount of bravery, intellect, resourcefulness, or beauty will change your fate."

With a shrug I stated the obvious. "I never really saw myself coming back from this party anyway, and it'll be enough to know I took you and all your pets out with me. Oh yes," I added with a smile. "I have also sent a detailed report to my handler, with proof of your existence so either way, your days are numbered."

"Americans, you are so fool hardy." He laughed loudly. "Your government knows about us, little miss, how do you think we replenish our numbers?"

His laughter drove me to take another step and I called out, "Bull-" My insult was cut short as I followed the sound of a rope being pulled tight. I thought I heard Alejandro's voice cry out a warning. The rope tightening around my ankles signaling it was too late to escape. I tried to activate the explosives, but the ground rushed to my head as my feet flew out from under me. I felt the impact of my skull on the ground and watched as the world around me faded to black.

CHAPTER ●———————— FIVE

I woke to the sound of Alejandro whispering my name, "Beau. Beau, are you alright?"

"How much did I drink? My head feels like it's in a vice." I groaned. My body felt odd, something wasn't right, but my head hurt too much to move. Pain seared through my skull when I opened my eyes and I knew I was in trouble. My training kicked in; instinctively I shut my eyes and examined my other senses. The room I was in smelt musty, slightly damp, and the scent of burning torches hung in the air. My hands and feet were bound and I was hanging by my arms. I tapped a foot, finding nothing beneath me. I sent my fingers searching, discovering a taunt rope above me. Muffled sounds found their way to me but I could only distinguish Alejandro's voice. My mouth was dry, and tasted like iron. I licked the side of my mouth, finding a trace of blood.

Alejandro murmured, "You hit your head pretty hard, try not to move."

"Cut me down and let's get out of here," I said. Opening my eyes ever so slowly, I tried to get my bearings. In front of me stood a stone wall. Enduring the pain, I twisted my body and found Alejandro trussed up three feet away. Unable to hide my disappointment I let out a sigh, earning an apologetic smirk.

With the tiniest of shrugs he teased, "At the moment that might prove difficult, but be patient we'll get out of here soon enough."

"I didn't realize you were so funny," I said with a roll of my eyes.

He smiled at me and replied, "Neither did I." Alejandro's body tensed, his eyes fixating beyond my shoulder, signaling we had company.

"Well, well, well what do we have here?" A heel slammed into my back, propelling me forward into Alejandro, the impact spinning me back to my original position till I was face to face with a tall, dark-skinned man. He sported odd green eyes and a shaved head - tribal tattoos running up one side of his scalp. He flashed a set of incredibly white teeth and snarled, "Is this the bitch that's been causing all the trouble?"

"Don't touch her," Alejandro warned.

I glared at my attacker, holding in my desire to kick him in the face and said, "That would be me, you Snipes wannabe."

His boot connected with my thigh, launching me into Alejandro for a second time as he roared, "Don't speak to me!"

"Don't touch her again." Alejandro growled.

Pulling my legs up to my waist, I pushed off of Alejandro, twisting on my return swing slamming my feet into my attacker's chest, knocking him into a shorter companion who stood at his side. "I'll speak whenever I damned well choose," I said flatly.

The vampire's eyes flared and turned ice green as he roared forward, his lips pulled back, bearing his fangs, snarling at me while his friend held him back, laughing. "Easy, Nevin. Uri says the boss wants to meet her."

"She killed Owen, she deserves a good beating at the very least," he said as he took another step forward.

Alejandro interjected, "You know he won't be happy if she's hurt."

The stubby redhead grinned and said, "He's right, Nevin, let's go." He nodded at me with a sideways sneer. "The boss will have something planned for her."

Nevin's green eyes flashed as he snarled. "When the boss is done with you, I'm going to make you pay for killing Owen."

With a crooked smiled I said, "You'll have to refresh my memory. I've killed a lot of people."

"B...," Alejandro caught himself. "Don't provoke him, I've little strength left."

"But it's so fun." I nodded at the redhead and

taunted, "Since you prefer your men short, I'm guessing the little runt I killed a couple of days ago was Owen." I tried to look bored as I continued, "He didn't put up much of a fight."

Alejandro let out a deep sigh behind me, whispering, "Why can't you stop?"

I clucked my tongue. "I'm starting to think you guys are only scary in fairytales and comic books. A kid fresh off the farm could have easily taken your runt...oh, pardon me...Owen. He was hardly worth my effort. I didn't even break a sweat."

Enraged, Nevin lunged at me, sending my body flying when he slapped my face. Blood oozing out of my mouth from the impact, I pushed my head upright and forced a smile to my lips and said, "You hit like a girl." I closed my eyes waiting for the coming blow, fairly certain it would reunite me with my father, but all I felt was gust of wind from behind.

The distinctive sounds of fists striking flesh drew my eyes open to find Alejandro straddling Nevin's body, growling. "I told you not to touch her!" The redhead sprawled out at his side, both seemingly unconscious.

For a moment I thought my last body slam had knocked Alejandro free, but the frayed ropes hanging from his still-bound wrists suggested otherwise. "Get me down and let's get out of here," I demanded.

Turning his face from me and holding up a hand, he whispered, "Beau, look away."

"Get me down," I insisted. He stood, but kept his back to me, spinning my body away as he lifted me up over the hook above. I felt his arms shake under the strain of my weight and I grew concerned and asked, "Are you hurt?"

His shoulders slumped forward as my feet reached the floor. He murmured, "I need time to recover, but I'll be fine." I pulled on his shoulders trying to get him to look at me so I could figure out where he'd been injured. "Don't look at me, Beau," he whispered, "I don't want you to see me this way."

"Don't be silly," I said as I tugged at his shoulder, but he pushed me away, reaching his arms over my shoulders, forcing my arms higher as he worked at the knots. The moment I was free I forced his chin toward me and asked, "Did you hit your head?" Immediately I jumped back, recognizing the ice blue change in his eyes. "You're one of them!"

Alejandro sank to the ground as if I had struck him, turning his head, attempting to hide the changes in his features. But it was too late, I had seen the proof. A chuckle behind me sent shivers up my spine. Turning, I found Uri with a wicked smile painted on his face as he gloated, "No, he is something...less." Uri growled down at his awakened men. "Get the hell up, I told you two not to get too close to him." He flicked a finger at me, commanding, "Re-secure them, tighter this time."

I moved to fight them off, but I could barely follow the blur of their movements, managing only a couple of lucky strikes. They overwhelmed us, and soon we were tied back to back and tossed into a corner. Nevin finished securing the ropes on my legs while his buddy hovered over Alejandro. The little redhead kicked Alejandro in the side, sneering at me. "Who's the runt now?"

"Quaid," barked Uri. Turning a smirk our way, Uri scoffed. "That's no way to treat our guests. After all, how sporting is it to kick a dog when he's down?"

Alejandro let out a half growl. "If any harm comes to her, Uri, I'm going to make you my next pet project."

His laughter boomed over us as he moved closer, kicking the sole of Alejandro's boot. "Look at yourself, spent and helpless, and for what? A human?"

"Untie me and I'll show you human," I said as kicked at him.

"Ooooh." He widened his eyes. "Scary." His men laughed at my expense, fueling my anger. Uri turned his eyes on Alejandro, and while crouching beside us, asked, "Why do you resist joining us? Why align yourself with these primitive people? I mean I see the attraction to this one; she's clever, and beautiful. But as one of us, she would be extraordinary."

"Don't even think about it," Alejandro warned him.

Uri leaned forward, catching a stray curl that had escaped my braid, pulling it close as he breathed in with a purr. "I bet you taste like warm honey."

Suddenly it dawned on me what he was referring to. I let my disgust drip from my tongue. "Get the hell away from me. I'd die before becoming what you are."

"Don't worry, he doesn't have the authority," Alejandro said with a smile. "Do you, Uri? For all your coveted power, you're still just an errand boy to your master."

Hatred burned in Uri's ice blue eyes as he asked, "And what are you? Nothing. You are nothing but a mere shadow of my master. You think you're better than us, better than he is, but you're weak and pathetic." Letting my curl fall free, his lips twisted over his words. "Make her your bride if you so desire, but take her blood rather than become paralyzed with exhaustion."

"I don't expect a man with your poor breeding

and limited intellect to understand the meaning of honor," Alejandro said dryly. "No, your role as lap dog becomes you rather nicely."

Uri whispered, "When the day comes that he wants you gone, I'll be the one that comes for you. I'm going to enjoy pulling the life out of your body drop by drop." Motioning to his men he stood with one last command, "Quaid, check on them every hour, make sure they stay tied up and keep the rest of the men out this area." He rammed a foot into Alejandro's shoulder, pushing him into the wall with a thud. "This one won't be a problem for a few hours, at least."

With a mocking sneer his men followed him out leaving us alone once again. Alone. Tied to a vampire. A vampire I had kissed – entertained having sex with. What would my father think of me now? Failure echoed in my head, my uncharacteristic recklessness rendered me captive and my mind was unable to calculate an escape.

He must have been following my thoughts because Alejandro whispered, "Beau, I am not one of them."

"Obviously, or I wouldn't be tied up with you."

He shook his head, clarifying. "I meant I am not a vampire."

"I saw you change with my own eyes, I know

what you are." I didn't bother to hide the distain in my voice. "Are you at least strong enough to free us?"

"No, I used all of my reserves." I felt him lean his head against the wall as he added, "But don't worry, my Shadow will soon find us."

Huffing out a breath, I asked, "What is that? Some kind of vampire code?" I lowered my voice, trying to mock his accent. "I'm a vampire that doesn't drink blood and is able to walk in the sunlight without SPF500. I move so fast it takes hours for my shadow to catch up to me, but when it finally does, I will command it to release my weak ass."

"Vulgarity doesn't become you, Beau," he said while attempting to turn his body toward me. "You can trust me."

"Every person I have ever trusted is dead, and soon I will join them. I knew this trip would be my end, but I had hoped to take a few more down," I admitted. Leaning back against Alejandro I asked, "If I let you take my blood, will you promise to kill as many of them as you can?"

Horrified he twisted toward me, digging the ropes into my flesh. I sucked in my pain as he bellowed, "I am not a vampire!"

"Can you turn back around?" I asked. Realizing

that I was in pain, he twisted back into place, providing much needed relief. As the pain subsided I sneered. "Thank you, Your Fangness."

"Not funny, Beau."

Taking a deep breath I admitted, "Sarcasm is my way of relieving stress, something I got from my father." I felt the muscles in his back relax as he leaned against the wall once more. "For the record, I don't think you're like them. I wouldn't have found you attractive," I said with a shrug, regretting the action immediately. "I have always been a good judge of character, but there's always the possibility that my initial instincts were wrong." I heard his breathing change and asked, "Are you seriously falling asleep?"

"I must recover before my Shadow arrives," he murmured.

Rolling my eyes I couldn't bite back the sarcasm. "Are you really going Peter Pan on me?" When he didn't respond I had to fight down the urge to jolt upward to wake him, instead I refocused my efforts toward escape. They had stripped me of my jacket but they left my vest on, slowly I worked my body toward my fingertips, straining till I reached the vest hem only to be denied. They had found my hidden throwing knife. Mentally I began checking off my tactical weapon list; coat and gloves were gone, my vest had been stripped, a quick flick of my fingers revealed they took my belt as well, leaving my pants and boots.

Looking down at the ropes binding my feet I sighed to myself. *"This is going to suck."* I could wait, giving Peter the non-vampire Pan his needed rest, or I could stop cutting him slack and wake his ass up. Memories of the way his lips felt against mine flooded my mind, his hand in the small of my back pulling me closer, the tingle in my abdomen as his eyes raked over my body. I sat upright, asking myself, *"What am I doing?"* I shook my head violently, trying to purge the unnerving images from my mind.

He stirred behind me and I froze, afraid for a moment that I had revealed my thoughts out loud. Silently, I prayed he had no idea how his kisses were haunting me. I was certain this attraction would pass. Feeling anxiety creeping up my spine, I turned my attention back to the problem at hand, not caring if he woke due the movement.

I twisted to the left, trying to roll onto my hip, hoping the pressure would tell me if a knife remained. Finding nothing, I began twisting to my right hip only to be denied once again. It had been a long shot any way, had I been the one conducting the search I would have found them as well. I sent up one final prayer then drove my heel into the ground, smiling at the welcome sound of my boot blade unsheathing. I would have found that as well, lucky for me Uri and his men underestimated me.

I would wait until the runt came to check on us since Uri had been foolish enough to give his orders in my presence. Rookie mistake- and he had the audacity to question my IQ? One by one I forced my muscles to relax, hoping to rest while I waited.

I found a strange comfort in the steady rhythm of Alejandro's breathing, and without thinking found myself in sync with the rise and fall of his chest. Slowly my eyes began to shut and I didn't fight them, I knew my lack of trust would keep my mind alert. It felt good, to have Alejandro at my back, even if it defied all logic. Still I couldn't disregard what I had seen, the image of his eyes turning ice blue and the budding eye teeth he had tried to hide, it was too fresh in my mind.

Searching my memory of Hollywood lore on vampires, I could only assume he was some type of hybrid since he was unaffected by the sun; if we made it out of here I would listen to his explanation then decide if he needed to die. The thought was depressing and immediately darkened my mood. My gut told me he was honorable – he was good. Even when his eyes turned to blue ice there had been warmth looking back at me, not the hard stares of Uri and his men.

His words crashed back into my mind, *"My sins and the sins of my family run far deeper and yet I still strive to serve good, to do what is right in the eyes of God"* No, every ounce of training and experience within me screamed he was a good, honorable man who I could trust. This wasn't a fight I could win with myself until I had the full picture so I tabled the topic for a later date. Hearing voices in the tunnels I dropped my head, pretending to be asleep like my co-captive.

"Aww, our two little lovebirds have managed to fall asleep." The squat leech rattled as he knelt down checking our ropes. Jerking the ropes tighter, he sneered. "Better sleep while you can, I have a feeling you'll be on the menu once the boss finds out what you've done." His hand brushed the top of my head. "What a waste, but Iliana would soon kill you. She never allows him to take a bride prettier than she is. Trust me it would be best if he allows us to kill you rather than deliver you into her hands." He leaned in, drawing in a deep breath. "You smell so good." The nearness of him made my skin crawl, making it difficult to maintain the guise of sleep. "If he allows us the chance, I will fight for the right to make you mine. He rarely allows us to take a woman, but your abilities might prove an exception." He chuckled as he stroked the side of my face. "One can hope." It was all I could do not to bite his fingers off, but I endured his sickening pawing, praying for his departure. He inhaled twice more before he stood, I could hear the smile in his voice. "You'll learn to appreciate me. It might take a few hundred years, but you'll come to respect me. I may be short but I'm faster than the others and I have other abilities. But for now I must go, dinner is waiting." Brushing his fingers over my lips he whispered, "I'll be back in an hour."

I waited till I could no longer hear the tread of his feet against the stone floor then slammed my heel down to free my knife. Twisting abruptly woke Alejandro. "Be still," he murmured.

"I'm afraid you'll have to sleep later, I need your help with my ropes." Scrunching and twisting till I got my boot knife under me I teased. "After I'm free you can get back to sleep if you want to stick around."

Discovering the blade in my boot he chuckled under his breath, "Why am I not surprised?" His elbow caught me in the ribs as he angled his hands over the blade. "Sorry."

Catching my breath from the unintentional blow, I muttered, "I have enough bruises at the moment, thank you." No matter how much he tried to avoid hurting me each pull of his ropes over the blade came with an elbow to my side and an apology. "For the love of God." I growled. "Quit pussy-footing around and cut the damned rope before you crack a rib."

"Fine, steady yourself and I will do one hard cut," he warned, looking back over his shoulder. I nodded at him to indicate I was ready and took a deep breath as his hands slid across the rope. I felt his hands come free bracing myself for the coming blow as his elbow slammed into my side. Despite my best effort my body slumped forward convulsing in pain, I whimpered but managed to contain my scream. "Try to breathe through the pain, Beau," he whispered as he pulled the ropes tighter reaching to work at the knot binding us back to back.

His body went still signaling there was a problem. Risking more pain I twisted to peek at what had made him stop, but I saw nothing in the dark passageway. A chirp relaxed Alejandro's shoulders as he let out a soft warble of his own. He leaned against me with another whisper, "My Shadow approaches."

Suddenly a dark-haired man stepped from the passageway, darting to Alejandro's side. A musty iron scent hit me full on, turning my stomach, threatening to relieve it of any remaining food. Our savior nodded down at me as he cut my bonds and asked dryly, "Can you walk?"

Try as I may I could not pinpoint his accent. "I can walk, run, or crawl," I said, looking up at him while trying not to breathe.

With a grimace he apologized. "Sorry about the smell, but it was my only way in." Alejandro stood, placing a hand on the man's shoulder, drawing his attention back to our escape. "We only have minutes," he said, nodding toward the passageway. "They're almost done eating. Can you flutter?"

Alejandro shook his head as he murmured, "Not yet, we will have to run till I recover."

With a sigh, the man produced a small tin from his pocket, opening the lid and holding it out with a warning, "A little goes a long way." Covering my face with a hand as the repulsive stench rolled over me, I took a step back. He pushed the tin toward me again, insisting. "Rub this over your clothes."

Alejandro rolled his eyes dipping his fingers in the red goo, rubbed his hands together then ran them over his body. Disgusted by the bombardment on my nasal cavity, I took another step back, shaking my head and said, "I'll pass, thank you."

The man chuckled at my displeasure but

Alejandro wasn't amused and insisted, "Do it, or I will do it for you." When I started to protest he explained. "They will track us, Beau, and this will throw off their scent. Now hurry; we have no time to waste."

Reluctantly I accepted my red goo, slathering it over my clothing as we crept down the passageway. "This is worse than a slaughterhouse, how long till your nose grows used to the smell?" I asked.

"It won't," our hero said with a smirk, as he brushed past to take lead. "It's made from the pheromones they produce after eating. Don't ask how I got it," he said with a final smile before he stared down a dark passage.

Alejandro turned, looking me in the eye, and firmly stated, "Stay with me, Beau. No matter what we see or hear, do not stop or leave my side."

His command raised my hackles. "I know when to fight and when to regroup," I said abruptly. He tried to take my hand but I shook him off with a hard stare. "I am not a child or some fair maiden needing rescue, just lead the way out."

I watched the silent rise and fall of the newcomer's shoulders as he held back his laughter. With a flick of his wrist he signaled for us to move to the passageway on the right then signaled for silence. Deftly he led us through the maze of seemingly endless passageways, looking back only to deliver directional signals.

As we neared the end of a pitch-black passage, a bluish glow burst into sight. Our leather-clad guide held up a hand to indicate for us to stop as he scouted ahead, clinging to the shadows of the open room lit with blue light. Alejandro turned his blue eyes on me and asked, "Once you are safe, will you give me a chance to explain?"

The hope in his eyes stirred unfamiliar feelings within me and I agreed without thought. "Yes."

"Thank you," he whispered. The corners of his mouth lifting to allow a slight smile, the sight made my knees weak and fear crept through my mind.

The reappearance of our guide allowed me to refocus on our escape, pushing my newfound emotions away. He crouched down besides us, looking intently at Alejandro, and said, "They are about to feed them." His eyes flicked toward me with a question. "Can she make it through without drawing attention?"

Irritated, I asked, "What's the problem?"

Alejandro pulled me close to keep his volume low as he answered. "We have to pass the Creeper pen and they are about to feed." His lips pulled back in disgust then he continued, "You cannot stop or draw attention to our position."

"I'm not going to scream like a girl," I said, not

hiding my irritation and pulling my arm from his grasp.

"The first time you see them..." He looked down at the ground, searching for the right words. "It can be unsettling to say the least."

Rolling my eyes at him I moved in behind our guide, proclaiming, "This isn't my first rodeo, I've seen blood plenty of times. Maybe I should fill you in on what I do for a living."

Alejandro gave a nod to our guide and we moved forward, sticking close to the uneven stone walls. I tried to curb my curiosity, but ever hungry for intel, my eyes found the sunken pen they spoke of and the things inhabiting it. Things indeed, because what I saw could barely pass as humanoid. Their grey bodies were huddled at the far corner near a wide door. They were snapping and growling at each other as they waited for their dinner to be delivered.

I did my best not to stare, to remain alert and on point, but the sight of their emaciated bodies skittering around the enclosure and over one another made every hair on my body stand straight up. Three quarters of the way across the room Alejandro pushed me into a dark nook, knocking my breath away. I cut off my rebuke when I heard the giant door groan open followed by the sinister laughter of the vampires bringing in the dinner.

"It would be best if you closed your eyes, the

nightly wager and feed isn't something you want to remember." Alejandro had barely spoken the warning as the first victim was dragged through the door. Two vampires held the horns of a majestic black bull as he tossed his head and kicked at his captors managing, for a brief moment, to dislodge the grasp of the vampire on the right.

"We have a fighter boys!" I heard Uri call out with a laugh. I followed his voice to a pack of men, cheering and waving their hands in the air. He pointed at a large chalkboard and one of his followers scribbling down a set of numbers. He twisted his head to look down at the now swarming Creepers. "As usual the house will back our less fortunate brothers two to one for the correct numbers of kills before their appetizer is finished; prizes to be paid tomorrow night."

The bull bellowed, tossing his head, trying to free himself, but the vampires proved too powerful. Three additional vampires approached the bull. One held what looked like two black glass horns high above his head. After the reinforcements immobilized the beast the black sheaths were cautiously attached to the tips of massive bull's own formidable set of horns, and he was loaded into a steel cage.

As the steel cage was lifted into the air a metal wall rose at the far side of the pit below. With the sound of the wall raising, the Creepers fanned out trumpeting and licking their lips in anticipation of what was to come. The sounds were deafening. The bull stomped the cage, tipping it side to side, snorting in fear at the smell of lay waiting beneath him. Horrified at the sight before me I pushed forward to stop this criminal display only to be pushed back and held to the wall by a sorrowful Alejandro.

I glared at him, growling. "Let me go."

"We cannot interfere," he said with a shake of his head. "At least they tip his horns with obsidian," he half-heartedly added. "I know you have questions, but they have to wait." He stared at me with sad eyes, keeping his back to the pit, refusing to look at the spectacle. "As much as it disgusts me, better the bulls than the townspeople."

"Two O negative for two kills," a voice cried out. The bidding had started and my heart sunk as knowledge they did this nightly sunk in. Each bet hurled out enraged my need for justice for every innocent life these vermin had taken, human and animal alike.

Uri yelled over the roar of his crowd, "Come on, guys, I need at least one risk taker tonight."

"Two AB negative for five," Nevin answered his challenge.

Uri smiled widely and said, "Now that's more like it."

His chalk-wielding assistant took a few more bets then announced the betting was closed. The vampires fanned out in a horseshoe pattern around the pit, chanting, "Down! Down! Down!"

Alejandro gave his dark-clad friend a nod and the man disappeared just as the wall shot back into the ground with an earthshaking thud. A Creeper leapt at the ground-pounding beast but the bull gored it in mid-air, leaving nothing but a grey ash to fall around the confused creature.

"One," Uri boomed out while the record keeper made note on the chalkboard.

I couldn't help but smile at the bull's victory, but the pity Alejandro wore on his face told me the worst was yet to come. The Creepers hugged the ground as they hissed and circled the beast, now hunting as a pack. The sudden pat on Alejandro's back caught me off guard, earning an apologetic smile from our guide whose head jerked to the side, signaling we could safely move on. As we moved toward the next passageway I saw the Creepers converge on the bull. Alejandro prodded me forward. With another quick shake of his head he said, "You cannot interfere without dying."

Reluctantly I turned down the passageway, closing my eyes as the sounds of the Creepers ripping the bull apart hit my ears. Unashamed, I let my guilty tears run down my face and whispered, "I should have stopped them."

CHAPTER ◆———— SIX

Moonlight spilt in ahead of us, marking the end of the tunnel. We were nearly out. Alejandro's hands flew over his ears, his eyes closed tightly as if shutting out an intense light then opened wide in alarm, even though I heard nothing. "They've sounded the siren," he explained.

Our guide nodded his head toward me, suggesting, "Her Jeep isn't far."

Alejandro's hand flew past me, grabbing his companion's coat, pulling him to a stop then he said, "No, they'll search there first, and we would be restricted to the road."

The dark-haired man ran his eyes over my gear while asking, "North, to the mountains?"

"I am willing to regroup," I interjected, "but I am not running." Alejandro's eyes widened in disbelief. "What?" I asked. "I have things in my room that can't really be explained. We can simply head back, invoke the treaty, and start over in a week or so."

With a shake of his head Alejandro dismissed my idea. "No, we cannot lead them back to town. They're hunting and will completely disregard the treaty," he said. His hand clasped over mine and he added decisively, "We go north into the mountains till they lose our scent." He didn't wait for an answer, simply pulled me out into the moonlight.

We ran in a zigzag pattern, trying to avoid bruising the vegetation or leaving our scent behind. Four klicks later Alejandro pulled me to the ground next to him, demanding, "Rest."

A canteen tapped at my shoulder as our rescuer smiled down at me, offering me a drink. He sat down on a nearby rock watching intently as Alejandro brushed the loose strands of my hair away from my face. His eyes lit up as he said, "Since Alejandro is being so rude I shall introduce myself."

"I apologize," Alejandro interjected. He waved a hand toward the dark-haired man and said, "Beau, this is Luken, my Shadow. Luken, this is Beau."

I stood abruptly staring down at his betrayal. "Really?" I demanded.

"There is no need to be angry with Alejandro," he said with a smile, "we harbor no secrets between us. And to be honest, I knew your name before he did, as you have a habit of talking to yourself when stressed." Luken tilted his head slightly letting his smile widen as he offered, "Pleasure to actually meet you, Beau."

"You've been following me," I stated flatly.

"Guilty as charged." His white teeth flashed in the moonlight as he said, "Though to be fair you're not easy to track and remain unseen. When did you discover me?"

Uncharacteristically I found myself instantly drawn to Luken, as if we had always and would always be friends. I returned his smile as I answered, "I felt more than saw you. You're extremely good at what you do."

"I am inclined to think the same of you." He teased. Sensing Alejandro's displeasure Luken gave a reluctant nod and added, "Excuse me, I want to circle back to be sure they don't have our scent."

Quizzically I asked, "Bodyguard?"

Before Alejandro could respond I heard a soft chuckle escape Luken as he drifted off in darkness. Alejandro's mood lightened and I could hear the smile in his voice. "I won't hear the end of that comment." He kept me waiting for the answer; too busy checking my body for injuries, much to my distain.

"I'm fine." I huffed when he wouldn't quit poking and prodding me.

Leaning back against a log, Alejandro gave me some space as he began his explanation. "Luken's family and mine are bound together in duty."

I queried, "So he is a family friend?"

His soft chuckle surprised me in the quiet night air. "He is far more than that," he confessed, "more like my brother than a friend. In fact, he is an extension of myself. I would have died long ago if not for him and the love of his family." A trumpeting sound in the distance shot Alejandro to his feet. From our left, Luken broke soundlessly from the trees. Alejandro seized my hand, pulling me toward Luken. "How close?" he asked.

"Two, maybe three, flutters," Luken said as his eyes darted my way. "They've given the hounds your scent."

"What's a flutter?" I asked.

Pacing back and forth, Alejandro ran a hand through his hair, cussing under his breath. "Damned Uri. He's always been too eager to please his master." With a deep sigh Alejandro slid his arm around my waist, pulling me tight to his chest, and said, "Remember you promised to give me a chance to explain, and I am holding you to it."

With a nod Luken launched himself onto Alejandro's back, winking at my surprise, then whispered, "Hold on tight, Killer."

Without any additional warning I felt my stomach rocket to my throat, cutting off my reply as we sprang up to a distant outcropping on the mountain. Never a fan of heights, I closed my eyes, trying to rationalize how we could have made the leap. The jagged edges of the rock face dug into my side as Alejandro shoved me into a crevice upon landing. My lips must have betrayed my pain because he brushed his lips over mine and whispered, "I'm sorry I hurt you."

His embrace made me dizzy but I managed to push him away, and said, "I'm fine." Then added dryly. "I suppose that was a 'flutter'."

Luken smiled warmly then crouched over the ledge, watching something below through a single spyglass. Plopping down next to him I followed the angle of his glass, trying to make out what he could be seeing. Pulling a finger to his lips he signaled for quiet then handed me the glass with a slow nod, guiding my sight to their position below.

The moment I acquired them in my sight they vanished. Confused, I grimaced at Luken, who simply smiled and readjusted my sight several miles north till I reacquired my target. Nevin was being pulled through the trees by the unseen hounds Luken had referred to, the grin on his face revealing his happiness to be in pursuit of his prey.

Directly behind him the second set of hounds burst through the thick underbrush, sending me scrambling backward at the sight. Two bloodless, pale bodies barely draped in rags snarled and clawed at each other, larger than the creepers in the pen we had seen. "Creepers with hyper-smell," Alejandro whispered at my shoulder. "They use them hunt down rogue soldiers and escapees."

Zeroing in for a closer look, I shivered at the sight of the enormous spiked collars fastened around their necks. I had a moment of pity for the people they once were and asked, "Who could create such a thing?"

"A selfish monster," Alejandro muttered as he turned away from the sight below.

Luken stood, offering his hand, and said, "Do not make the mistake of thinking of them as people any longer, Beau." I let him draw me to me feet, handing back his glass. "If they get your scent they'll tear you to pieces without an ounce of regret."

"Come," Alejandro said as he held out his hand. "They'll find our last position and have our scent any moment." As Luken leapt to his back Alejandro called back to him, "Two jumps then you circle back for Beau's things; I'll take her to our east camp."

Luken slapped his shoulder twice conveying his understanding while Alejandro pulled me tight to his chest. Our feet had no sooner left the ground than I heard the Creepers let out a wailing trumpet, discovering our scent just as he had predicted. Feeling sick as my stomach reacted to this new form of travel, I squeezed my eyes shut.

With a half-hearted smirk Luken informed me, "Keep your eyes open, Killer, it's worse if you don't."

The tree line sped past me at a dizzying rate, leading me to doubt his words of wisdom. "Easy for you to say since you can see what's coming at you, I only have your mug to look at." His laughter earned a bark from Alejandro and we shared a smile at his rebuke.

Alejandro's feet slammed into the ground, jarring my bones with the impact and we were off again. My stomach stopped fluttering with each passing tree and I smiled at the faces Luken was making as he tried to take my mind off the hair-raising ride. I watched Luken slip off of Alejandro's back with the next impact, waving silently as Alejandro launched forward without pause.

Two jumps later found us battered to a stop, my body absorbing a gauntlet of unrelenting contact with whipping arms that sliced into my flesh. My head hummed with the impact of something solid at my temple, bringing an odd relief as my body settled into a spent ball, unable to move another inch while the smell of freshly disturbed earth filled my nose.

"Beau," Alejandro called softly. "Beau, are you hurt?"

Trying to reassure his frantic inquiry I forced myself to respond, "I'm fine, and frankly glad to be on the ground." Pulling body upright I realized we were in a cornfield. Laughter rocked my sides as I pictured the ears of corn pounding us to a stop rather than the fists of Nevin and his short little buddy as I had feared. I laughed harder as Alejandro fixed his eyes on mine. *He must think I am insane*, I thought to myself. I smiled at him, teasing, "Just so you know, I'm never going on vacation with you. The flights are definitely lacking in customer service."

Collapsing on the ground in relief, he gave into his laughter. He replied, "I'll have you know I'm an excellent pilot."

"Wow. Your landings get worse than that?" I dug my hand into the soil and flung the dirt his way, and asked, "Perhaps our next date will end with me in the hospital?"

"How presumptuous!" He chuckled. "We first have to ensure we live before I can ask you out on a proper date, my lady." Sitting up he brushed the dirt off his coat, staring intently at me. "Are you sure you're unharmed?"

"A few scrapes and cuts. Had I known you were taking me to visit the Children of the Corn I would have packed a first aid kit," I said.

Instantly he was at my side, running his fingers over the cuts on my arms. "Now I know you're hurt; you often turn to humor to cover your pain."

Irritated that he discovered a tell, I pulled my arm back, declaring, "I am fine."

Reluctantly he relinquished my arm, and said, "Have it your way, but once we get to the camp you're going to be looked over."

I took my time getting to my feet to obscure any additional signs of pain, casually saying, "I should be good to go from here. I'll get my bearings and go back to get my things from Luken." Bending over to brush the dirt from my legs was a mistake that he didn't miss, catching me in his arms as I toppled forward.

"You're staying with me," he said with a sigh. "Luken will bring anything you need to the camp after he ensures they have lost our scent."

Trying to change the subject, I asked, "Do you have any other abilities I should know about, or are you simply going to spring them on me one at a time?"

"I will explain what I am able once you're safe," he said as he pulled corn husks out of his sleeve. "I need a few minutes to recover then two last flutters should put us in range of the camp." Pulling a small flask from his coat he took a swig of the contents, putting it away without offering me a drink.

Tilting my head at him in annoyance, I muttered, "I thought you were a gentleman."

"I am sorry, Beau, but this wouldn't agree with you. There will be water at the camp." His eyes narrowed as he guessed what was running through my mind. "It is not blood!"

I rolled my eyes, shrugging my shoulders then offered, "Whatever."

"Fine, take a drink but you won't like it," he said as he thrust the flask at me.

Defiantly I took a sip earning a deep chortle as the bitterness of the drink contorted my features. "That's disgusting." I coughed, returning the vile liquid to its proper owner. "You can keep it."

"I did warn you." His lips twisted as he spoke. "It is an acquired taste. Luken's wife steeps bitters for me, it speeds my recovery time."

Pulling back my lips in disgust, I replied, "I would recover quickly just to avoid another sip."

He smiled, shaking his head as he tried to contain a chuckle. "Luken's people will be at the camp," he said then paused, searching his mind for the right words. "They take their time warming up to outsiders. Many of them still refuse to speak to me, and our families have been bound for more time than I have bothered to count. We should not expect a joyous welcome."

"I prefer the silent type over people intent on becoming my best friend," I replied as I took my position in his arms for the next flutter. I looked up at him from beneath my lashes, and said, "Although,

I might consider a friendship if they offer me a warm meal."

He pulled me tight to his chest as he bent down, claiming my lips. His hunger made my head spin, stirring something within me, something foreign and uncomfortable. Releasing my lips, he whispered, "You will be denied nothing." I felt his arms tighten and the ground fell away from my feet.

A second jump found us on the outskirts of what could only be described as a gypsy caravan minus the stereotypical bright colors. We received a few head nods but no one seemed surprised by our sudden appearance. Taking my hand in his, Alejandro pulled me toward a large wagon near the center of the circle. The young girl at the campfire served Alejandro first then filled a bowl and handed it to me with a shy smile.

I returned her smile accepting the steaming bowl of stew, and said, "Thank you."

The girl looked quickly around her then leaned forward, whispering, "Did you really kill eight vampires?"

Blinking back my surprise at her knowledge of recent events, I barely managed to squeak out a reply, "Umm...yes."

Her big brown eyes sparkled with admiration. "Not even the men hunt the demons," she said.

"She got lucky, Izar," Alejandro warned with a stern look. "Do not let such thoughts linger in your mind."

"Izar." A woman stood beckoning the girl. "Back to your chores." I watched as the girl grudgingly walked toward the woman who wore her hair pulled back in a tight bun. The older woman ran her eyes over me, not bothering to hide her disgust, then let out a string of what could only be described as rebukes in a tongue I had never heard before.

Alejandro let out a sigh. "That is Knotxesi, the matriarch of the clan. I apologize for her rudeness. I would like to say it will not happen again, but she does not play well with others on a good day, and you pose a threat to their way of life."

"I don't even know them," I said quizzically. "How could I be a threat?"

He motioned toward the girl peeking over her shoulder at us again, and explained, "Izar idolizes you, she hangs on Luken's every word when he speaks of you and that frightens Knotxesi. Izar is not clinging to the old ways the way the other young ladies are, she is far too inquisitive and seeks out things of this era."

I shook my head, and stated, "I don't see the problem."

"They are Basque Roma," he said abruptly. I stared at him, waiting for further explanation, and he chuckled at my ignorance. "There are few traditional Roma clans living today that cling to the old ways, still speak the old tongue, and they want their children to keep their heritage alive." He reached forward, setting his empty bowl near the fire then continued, "Strong, passionate, outsider women like you pose a threat to future generations of Roma women. You will not find many within the clan that will speak to you, let alone want you to speak to their children."

My brows came together in irritation as I asked, "So they force their daughters into subservient roles? That is positively archaic."

"Would the world be better if everyone believed as you do?" His eyes flashed with sarcasm as he chided, "Or do your beliefs allow for others to retain the right to hold onto traditions that are the foundations of a culture you know nothing about, nor are in a position to judge?

I felt my jaw set defiantly as my words spilt out colder than intended. "I am all for tradition as long as each individual is given the choice to embrace it on their own, not be brainwashed or forced into a role that limits their dreams."

"Point taken, but you are forgetting a parent's duty to raise their child on a firm foundation so the prevailing winds of life do not push them into harm."

He smiled and probed. "Did your father not ensure you had a firm foundation on which to stand?"

Stacking my bowl on his, my lips twisted out my response. "Yes, I am definitely the woman I am today because of the way my father raised me."

He asked, "And do you like who you have become?"

"Yes," I admitted. "I see your point and apologize for being quick to judge."

He tilted his head to the side, and said, "No apology needed, I simply want you to reserve judgment until you have a chance to understand their ways. They are a noble people and a child could do far worse than to grow up with the love of an entire clan and their ideals."

"Enough about my flaws," I said while shifting my weight to get more comfortable. "Tell me why you can do the things you do if you aren't one of them."

"Long or short story?" he asked.

I let out a deep breath, and asked, "Are we going anywhere tonight?"

"No," he said flatly. Poking the campfire with a stick he avoided my stare, obviously stalling and deepening my irritation of being kept in the dark. Feeling my stare boring into him he turned and said, "This would be easier if you trusted me enough to simply show you."

"In case you haven't noticed, I have trusted you with my life for the last twenty-four hours." My revelation earned a disarming smile. The sensation forced me to break eye contact. Trying to change the subject, I brought him back to point, asking, "How are you going to show me?"

His hand slid inside his jacket retrieving a tiny blue velvet bag. "This contains the blood memories of my grandfather," he whispered as he opened the bag, producing a gleaming silver tin. "I brought this from home intending to teach Gau." His eyes fixed on mine. "Luken's son, but he can wait a few more days. At the moment your explanation takes priority."

"Blood memories?" I asked.

The corners of his mouth lifted. "Yes, a small amount of blood contains every memory prior to the day the drop was given and when mixed with the right herbs we can share those memories with others such as yourself," he stated. "Without proper guidance, the images can jumble, blur and become nightmarish, leaving one disoriented at the least. It's even possible to leave a specific message within the blood if one is skilled enough to focus the thoughts into a narrative."

My nose wrinkled up involuntarily as I questioned, "Is it safe?"

"Quite," he assured me with a chuckle. Kneeling

at my side, he continued, "The fastest way to the truth is under the tongue, but if the thought is too displeasing I can mix it in a glass of wine." I opened my mouth and lifted my tongue, letting him shake the powder out of the tin. He smiled reassuringly and said, "Sit back, close your eyes, and let my voice guide you through his memories."

Skeptical, I leaned against the log at my back and closed my eyes, expecting nothing to happen while I waited for the iron taste of the dried blood to fade. The sound of metal striking metal shot my body upright. My hand automatically flew to my waist, but came up empty.

"Beau," Alejandro whispered, "it is a memory. You are safe here, sit and try to relax." Unconvinced I let my eyes judge for myself, but found no lurking threat. A gentle hand touched my wrist as he said, "Please sit, I promise to alert you if there is a need." A sound jerked my head to the left but I let him pull me back to the ground. "The memories will be erratic at first. You will be seeing through his eyes, feeling what he felt, but you must remember these are nothing but his memories, not your own, and you are safe."

Jumbled images assaulted my mind, some terrifying, while others were tender and heart breaking. Alejandro's voice reached my ears as I struggled to regain control of my reeling head. "Do not resist the memories," he said softly, "focus on the sound of my voice and let it guide you. Trust my voice; I will not leave your side." He slid his hand in mine, and I forced my body to relax.

"It is the year of our Lord, 845." Amid the flurry of images I tried to focus on Alejandro's voice and the specific words he was using. "You have been charged to serve the Church in the *Reconquista* and eradicate the Love of Death Warriors - the Moors' newest weapon."

Suddenly a massive field stretched out in front of me, the stench of death filling my nose. A wide-eyed warrior with a curved sword ran toward me, screaming in a language I could not understand. Waiting until the last possible moment, I lunged to my right spinning on my heel as I followed his momentum, and thrust my blade into his exposed side. His death saddened me but I had no time to dwell on my feelings for another had taken his place, swinging wildly as he screamed toward me.

Alejandro urged me. "Move forward in time, concentrating on your family, look for your children." *In the distance, the sound of a babbling creek caught my attention and I turned, following the sound. A forest replaced the battlefield and love filled my heart, driving the smell of battle far away as my three sons ran toward me, a string of fish in each of their hands.*

Their smiles and laughter seared through me filling me with pride and a need to see my beautiful wife, Pascuala.

"Your wife needs you," Alejandro whispered. *I reached out for her as she extended a frail, weathered hand and I brought it to my lips as I sat upon our bed. The trees of the forest gave way to the stone walls of our family home as I gathered her frail, elderly body in my arms. No comfort was found in the eyes of my bishop, nor the physician I had summoned. My sons, now grown men, fanned the end of our bed unashamed of the tears they were shedding with the knowledge their mother was leaving this world.*

Alejandro's voice grew sorrowful. "Let your mind recall the day she died, when you were visited by Vasco Sanchez." *The air around me grew cold and I could see my breath form in the air before me as I prayed heart-broken over my bride one last time, and begged her to wait for me in heaven. My sons' footsteps faded behind me as they escorted those in mourning from the great hall to give me a few last moments with my love. I caressed the side of her face, picturing her in the glory days of her youth, recalling the evenings I spent watching her brush her long dark locks.*

Slowly I slid the obsidian inlaid brush I gave her when our first son was born into her folded hands.

"You are so beautiful, my love," I whispered as I kissed her fingers one last time. I turned the matching looking glass around in my hand, staring at my reflection. A woe-filled face stared back at me, still in the prime of my life, barely aging despite the many years that had passed since I took Pascuala as my bride. I had betrayed her by not growing old at her side, never knowing when I would die and rejoin her in the heavens.

I moved the glass, intent on placing it in her hands only to freeze as the sinister reflection of Vasco Sanchez came into view. Gently I finished my movement, struggling to maintain my duty to honor my wife and slid the looking glass into her hands. "Have you come to kill me?" I asked the man looming in the background.

He let out a malignant cackle. "No, I have come to witness the pain of your loss."

"If you did not come to end my suffering leave me." I turned to face him, declaring, "Brujo's are not welcome here, nor will I allow your filthy eyes to gaze upon my bride."

"She was promised to me," he hissed.

"You were unworthy of her!" I snapped.

"And you were?" Vasco Sanchez circled me.

My head dropped as I admitted, "Her love made me worthy."

Vasco pointed his wand hatefully at me. "Know

this, it was I that cursed you; cursed you to forever feel the pain you inflicted upon me when you stole what belonged to me. The pain and emptiness you feel pounding in your chest will follow you throughout the ages, for you are condemned to life – life without her. I have deepened your senses, allowed you to feel to your core, unhindered, and as your loss will never fade, you will never love again. Your life extends my own and your pain feeds my strength." His laughter sent chills down my spine as the reason for my agelessness crowed before me.

Enraged, I charged him. Blow after blow met only air as he laughed and danced around me. "You cannot harm me, you ignorant fool." He chortled. "My curse prevents you."

"To arms," I screamed for my sons. They charged into the room to stand at my side. My eyes narrowed upon the witch. "Then my sons will kill you," I assured him.

The bishop wobbled in behind us, saw Vasco and immediately commanded, "Kill the brujo!" My sons rushed forward, causing Vasco to leap through the window. We watched as his body transformed into a raven and flew east, denying us our victory.

"Beau," Alejandro called to me from the distance, "let go of the memories and come back to me."

I hugged my sons to my chest, broken from my loss and finding no lasting comfort, dwelling on the

words of Vasco Sanchez and the knowledge my love
for their mother may have passed my curse down my
bloodline. I heard Alejandro's voice call to me again
and I followed it as the world around me shattered
into small pieces, only the deep loss remaining.

Alejandro's fingers wiped the tears from my face
as I sobbed into his chest. "He loved her so much."

"Yes, he did, and his sorrow made Vasco a very
powerful brujo," he said. "Until my father was able to
end him." Alejandro rocked me in his arms, fully
aware of the emotional connection I still had with his
grandfather. I clung to him, my body wracked by the
pain of his loss. "His feelings will fade, Beau, and
soon you will be yourself once again." The vivid
emotions drained me of all energy and I was grateful
to be wrapped in the safety of his strong arms.

Alejandro ran his fingers through my hair,
pulling my head further into his chest. "My
grandfather relayed the entire conversation to the
bishop, but the Church was unable to break the
curse." Alejandro's voice grew low. "He begged the
priests to end his suffering for years, but they
informed him the curse was a sign that his family
was meant to serve God in the crusade."

"The curse not only deepened his ability to feel,
but imparted other heightened senses and abilities
such as speed, strength, and agility. The energy cost
was high though, and made long battles difficult as

their power waned with each thrust of the sword," he continued as he held me tight. "My grandfather and his sons began fighting in teams of two, back to back, allowing one to rest as the other fought. That is, until the Church discovered an answer and presented our family with Blessed Bloodstone Amulets that strengthened us and gave us clarity of mind, allowing us to face any enemy without growing weak during the battle."

I recalled how spent his body was when we were tied up, and asked, "Did you lose yours?"

"This was hundreds of years ago, their power eventually waned and the bishops that held the secret of their power are long since dead," he stated. I tried to sit up, but he held me in place. "Not just yet." His fingers brushed the side of my face as he whispered, "Let me enjoy you for a moment longer while your body recovers."

Settling down with my head on his chest, I asked, "Will you tell me more?"

His hand caressed my arm as he continued, "I was born in 1353, and I, like my father and my siblings, inherited my grandfather's curse and duty to the church. They called us Bloodknights." His voice grew sad and distant, "Demons have walked this earth since the beginning of time in various shapes, with varying abilities and intentions. My family has served over the centuries, dedicated to protecting the innocent, but my family has also done unspeakable harm."

I sat up, wanting to see his face when I inquired, "What happened?"

He looked away in disgust, and said, "My brother discovered the power of blood."

"Is that what you meant by the sins of your family?" I asked.

"Yes," he admitted. "It was quite by accident the first time. We were fighting and blood sprayed into his mouth, he surged with power, moving faster than I had ever seen before. He fought the desire for the same rush for years, but eventually gave in and began secretly bloodletting prior to battle. Eventually he became addicted, and his unclean habit spawned what you now call vampires."

I shook my head, and said, "I don't know what to say."

"The blame is mine. I kept his secret, a secret that cost me my family. Only my mother, brother and I remain. She is locked away in her grief, only strands away from death, and my brother is in exile." His lips twisted in pain, "I have not the strength to end his life."

I turned his chin to make him look at me, knowing no matter my father's crime I would defend him to the death rather than allow someone to take his life. "No one should be forced to kill their family," I said firmly. I watched the struggle between the love for his brother and his need to protect the innocent stir within him, and I realize for once in my life not all decisions were black and white. I regretted my previous quick judgments. What would I really do if it were my father at the heart of this death? I lowered my voice, trying to convey my limited understanding of his struggle. "No one should ever ask that of someone."

His guilt-ridden eyes pierced my heart as he whispered, "At what cost? How many should die for the love of my brother?"

CHAPTER ●———— SEVEN

The next morning Luken was sitting at the fire with a smile when I woke. "Care for some breakfast?" he asked.

"You read my mind, I'm starving," I said as I stretched. Expecting to find Alejandro on the bedroll next to me I let my hand drop, but came up empty.

Luken handed me a plate of cheese, bread, and fruit with a knowing smile, stating, "He should be back any time."

I stretched again to cover my former action. With a yawn, I asked, "Who?"

"The only ones you're fooling are yourselves." He laughed. "But I can play along if it brings you comfort."

I spread the fresh cheese over my bread avoiding eye contact when I replied, "I'm sure if I knew what you were talking about I might be irritated." I fixed my eyes on his, adding, "People don't usually like me when I'm irritated."

His laughter drew stares from the men busy packing up the camp. "Settle down, killer, I have no intention of ending up on your list." Walking toward me he dropped one of my bags at my feet. "I believe Alejandro finalized your stay at Diego's and had your Jeep returned so you've no need to go back."

Shoving a few grapes into my mouth I dug in my bag to see what he had retrieved. On the top were both of my passports. "Hmmm, you are thorough, aren't you?" I inquired.

"I only grabbed the essentials," he said with a sideways smile.

"My laptop, cash, phone, weapons, and what is this?" I pulled out a blue envelope. Luken squinted down at me, shifting his weight as I opened the envelope finding a one-way ticket. "So, I live in Arizona now? I'm sure you're aware they won't exactly welcome me at the airport with these weapons."

He kicked at the dirt, looking around the camp to be sure we weren't overheard before he answered, "I tried to tell him you would resist and I would appreciate it if you don't tell him I returned the weapons and your body armor." I held up a package, earning another twisted smile. "Enough dried beef for a week," he said slyly. As I dug deeper he let out a sigh of annoyance. "All of the weapons, including those that were hidden." I smiled at his efficiency but he didn't return it. He ran a hand over his well-groomed beard. "He will be angry with me, but if you do what I think you are going to do...you will need them. And his wrath would be greater if I let you go unarmed and you were hurt."

"Thank you, Luken, but I can't leave here until I finish this," I declared.

His lips twisted over his words, "I was afraid you would insist on staying, but I hoped you'd listen to reason." A black blade sliced into the ground between my legs. "You'll need that as well. It's an obsidian blade for Creepers. Stick them anywhere. As long as the glass punctures the flesh they will die. You are a skilled fighter, Beau, but your humanity is no match for them. Eventually your luck will run out."

I studied the blade and asked, "Is this what they placed on the bull's horns?" He nodded sadly at the memory we shared of the Creepers' dinner. "My father used to say only a fool relies on luck," I said, while zipping up my bag and sheathing my new blade. Handing him my empty plate, I asked, "Do I look like a fool?"

The corners of his mouth lifted slightly as he answered, "No, you look like the first outsider I have ever cared if they killed." His face grew serious. "Please listen to Alejandro and consider those you killed as payment for the death of your friends. Your current course of action will lead to your death or worse, change you into that which you hate."

Swinging the bag over my shoulder I gave him one last smile. "One day maybe you will understand

I do the things I do for the greater good." I said as I shook my head while handing him the unwanted blue envelope. "Sometimes I let revenge fuel my actions, but just as you want your children to follow in your footsteps I must follow my father's path. He stood for those that could not stand for themselves, protected the innocent, and served his country even when it was unappreciated." I placed my hand on his shoulder gripping it tight. "Thank you, Luken, for all that you've done for me, you're a good man. Take care of our mutual friend."

"He will want to say good-bye," he said with a sly grin.

"I'm not good at good-bye," I admitted. He nodded his understanding and I turned west knowing I had to set a brisk pace to find cover before nightfall.

Every four klicks I changed direction hoping to avoid Alejandro picking up my trail with thoughts of forcing me to make that flight. The hike gave me time to process my options. My first thought was to head back and blow my charges. I was certain they were unable to disarm them and they undoubtedly believe I'm running for my life so may not have given them a second thought. That would likely lead to them to move to another base of operations. How long would it take for me to relocate them? I shook my head at the thought of losing them for months. No, I'll save that surprise for the right moment.

I could walk away clean as Luken suggested, simply claim the eight lives for the two they stole from me, but there was no way I could live with myself if I left these things alive – free to feed off innocents. And then there was the adrenalin rush, taking these things down pumped a bigger high than taking down a cartel. Reason enough to stay on target. No, walking away was out of the question.

My best chance at survival would be to employ guerrilla tactics - engaging them at their weakest points, harassing them when their guard was down, and using their inflated egos to my advantage. I would study them, making my strikes count and defeat them with a long game. What else did I have to do? I could take odd jobs for Conrad to fund my need for weapons, or perhaps I could find a cartel operating down here to periodically raid for supplies. I smiled at the latter thought; this could prove quite rewarding.

As a plan began to take form, I decided to head north far past my target. Later, I would backtrack through the mountains and set up a mobile base camp. It was a relatively solid plan and should afford me enough obscurity to set up my surveillance with low risk of exposure.

The coming weeks proved to be the best adrenalin high I had ever experienced, I was completely addicted to this new hunt. Sure, I had a few close calls, but each near death experience made me a better hunter. Luken discovered my sweep pattern two weeks in and though I never saw him, the bundles left in my camp could have only come from him. They solved my need for weapons and supplies and often included the vile red goo to mask my scent. I could only speculate that he had not informed Alejandro of my actions as Alejandro never showed up to voice his disapproval or deliver a lecture on the need for me to return home.

Home. As if I had one since my father died. I did return stateside three weeks into my assault. To ensure I didn't establish a pattern the vampires could begin to anticipate. I used the time to see Ji and add a few new petals. Ji seemed surprised that I asked for a new color, but he was wise enough not to press me for more information. And how exactly would I explain I wanted the new color to mark my vampire kills – he would think I was crazy. The new dark pink petals seemed almost destined for my tattoo, making the light pink pop out more.

Once that was done I returned to my task, continuing to vary my attacks, avoiding obvious patterns, and attempting to do the most damage when I did strike. My first thought had been to disrupt their food supply, but I was afraid if I hit the mobile blood drive Uri would take it out on the town. Even though it sickened me, I had to admit Alejandro was right to broker the deal that saved the town from out-right attack.

It was clear there was a pecking order of sorts among the ranks, much like our military. And why not? I was certain many of the vampires I had observed had military training. Uri seemed to be in charge of this base and was taking some heat over the losses I had inflicted. Two different late-night convoys had rolled in, greeted by a tight-lipped Uri, but my vantage point didn't deliver the right angle to see who the VIPs were.

When the convoy returned for the third time I decided I needed more intel. Hopeful that I might finally get eyes on the leader of this group, I smeared a thick layer of Luken's disgusting blood salve over my clothes, loaded up my gear, and headed in for a closer look. It had been over a week since my last attack, in which I had managed to cause major damage by letting the Creepers loose inside the base.

I waited for dinner time, took a deep breath and slid into the back cavern. Twenty feet in I began to seriously doubt the wisdom behind the choice to re-enter these caves. Hugging the wet stone walls, I prayed for Luken's ability to meld into the shadows as a sentry passed. The vampire, clearly irritated to be working while the others were eating, walked past me without missing a stride. I bit back my grin, happy to have killed enough of them to warrant the new patrols, but irritated by my lack of knowledge of this change prior to my trip into the lion's den.

Passing another marking on the wall I took the next passageway toward the Creepers' pen, carefully navigating by the fluorescent chalk marks I had left on my last scouting trip. Weaving my way through the passageways carefully, I came to the end of my chalking forays, a three-pronged fork in the caves waited for my decision. With the addition of the new patrols I knew the smartest move was to wait, watch, and memorize the patrol patterns. The problem with waiting was I had no idea if the entourage that had arrived today would be staying long enough for me to get a look at them. No, I had to take the risk – I had to get eyes on the leader. I waited for the patrol in front of me to pass then darted for the center passage, clinging to the shadows as I ventured into the unknown.

I didn't have to go far before sounds of movement echoed the presence of at least two guards at the opening of the next room. Picking each step carefully, I pushed myself into the wall, inching closer to the sounds ahead.

"She can't be stupid enough to come in here," an unfamiliar voice grumbled. "I don't see the need for this amount of security. After all, there is only one of her and all of us. She got lucky last time, letting the Creepers out – lucky they didn't get a hold of her." The unknown voice belonged to the sentry which had just passed me in the hall. "Now I have to wait to eat, it's bullshit!"

Nevin's unmistakable voice growled, "Quit whining!"

Hugging the wall tighter while crouching down, I waited in the darkness trying to determine if they were moving, instead a third voice joined their conversation. The all-too-familiar sound of the red runt's voice reached my ears. "What's he going on about now?"

"The usual." Nevin sneered. "I think he is allergic to work." From my crouched position, I watched the redhead, Quaid, enter the room. Spotting the gift in Quaid's hand Nevin, slapped his hands together and held them out in anticipation as Quaid tossed him a pint of blood. "Sweet, I'm starving," he said with appreciation.

"Hey, where's mine?" the sentry whined.

Quaid looked back at the sentry with a shrug. "Do I look like your mommy?"

"Worthless," the unknown sentry muttered as he leaned against the stone of the cavern not bothering to hide his loathing.

"So what are you grumbling about now?" Quaid murmured as he hopped up on the crate next to Nevin. The sight of the two of them sitting back nonchalantly drinking a pint of blood made me want to heave; they needed to be erased – eradicated. The world would be better without them in it.

Nevin answered for their companion. "He's pissed we have to be on guard duty."

"She's human for crap sake, and a woman!" The sentry exclaimed. Quaid and Nevin snickered while shoving one another back and forth, obviously sharing a laugh at the newcomer's expense. "Fine, she killed a few of us. So what? She got lucky!"

Quaid pushed his lips into a fake frown and nodded rapidly as he inquired, "So then...you'll be fine if we lock you in a room with her alone when we catch her?"

Nevin elbowed Quaid, adding with a snicker, "I'd pay to see that, maybe then we could get some peace and quiet."

The vampire glared at the two laughing at his expense. "Without her sneaky little tricks, she's no match for any of us one-on-one," he said with a sneer.

In the blink of an eye Nevin had the vampire pinned against the wall with his hand clasped around his neck, no trace of a smile left on his face. "Are you suggesting Owen was weak?" He growled. The vampire kicked and clawed to no avail. Nevin shoved him against the wall once more, asking, "Well? Are you?"

Quaid put his hand on his friend's elbow to calm him, and said half-heartedly, "He might answer if you let him get some air." He looked up at the helpless vampire. "Blink twice if you didn't mean to imply Owen was weaker than you."

From my vantage point I couldn't make out if he was complying; besides I was far more interested in the room Quaid had exited. Let the two bloodsuckers kill each other, less for me to clean up later. So enthralled in finding a path to the door on the opposite side of the room I didn't notice the absence of the redhead until he was at my side.

"Get out of here," he whispered. I stared at him, blinking back my shock that he hadn't sounded the alarm. Quaid shook my arm and whispered once more, "Get out of here while you can. If they see you I'll have no choice but to catch you." My eyes darted back to Nevin still growling at the complainer pinned against the wall. Quaid pulled me away from the room. "What is wrong with you? Get out of here or you'll either be dinner or become a plaything. Is that what you want?"

Confused by his behavior, I asked, "Why would you help me?"

He brushed a stray curl away from my face and I tried not to flinch from his touch. "I've come to respect your persistence, strength, and of course your, beauty. The thought of you turned into a Creeper is distasteful to say the least," he said softly. "You are far too extraordinary a creature to risk turning."

The image of myself gaunt and bloodless was almost as disgusting as the knowledge he found me attractive. I shoved him away from me as I demanded, "Back off, small fry."

Undaunted, he smiled wide and offered, "I told you my other talents make up for my height. Am I really too short for you?" He asked as he began pulling me down the passageway once again. His vice-like grip on my arm reminding me not to assume I would easily free myself.

I sneered. "I prefer my men without fangs, thank you."

He asked, "So, I was wrong to believe you and Alejandro were an item?" His hopeful smile made me sick, and I was unable to resist shoving him into the opposite wall. "Giggity, giggity," he whispered.

Disgusted by his sexual arousal I shoved my forearm into his throat. "Listen to me, little beast. I would never have anything to do with someone involved in the death of my friends," I assured him.

"And yet you can't take your hands off me," he replied with a twisted smile.

Unable to hold my anger in any longer, I let my frustration out. "Aaagghhh, I have never met a more annoying individual!"

Quaid's smile disappeared. "Run," he whispered.

Instantly I realized the folly of allowing my frustration to make me forget exactly where I was and what detection could mean. I heard shouting coming from the passageway to my right and quickly tried to get my bearings. Quaid latched onto my shoulder and fluttered us down a tunnel just as I realized we had made our way back to the fork where I had made the decision to take the center passage. We landed against a wall, driving the air from my lungs. When I looked up he was gone.

Struggling for breath I pulled myself upright trying to determine where I was and praying I could somehow make it out of the caves alive. Every breath I took sliced through me signaling I had cracked or broken a rib. Forcing the pain from my mind I focused on finding a chalk mark while moving as quietly as possible.

In mere heartbeats Quaid returned, pointing a finger down the passage. "Take the next left, it will lead you out," he said quietly. I shook my head in understanding, mouthing a thank-you while trying to contain the pain the subtle action induced. His brows came together in worry. "Did I hurt you?" He leaned in and took a deep breath. "Oh my God, you're bleeding." He turned, running his hand through his hair as he shook his head, pacing back and forth while having an internal conversation.

I didn't wait to hear the outcome, forcing my feet to take the path he had directed. I promised my body it could rest once I was clear. I felt Quaid's hand grasp my shoulder just as a gush of air forced me into the wall with another painful thud. I turned my head to find Alejandro raining blows upon my would-be protector until Quaid lay limp at his feet.

Alejandro stood shaking his head, whispering, "Why? Why would you risk this?"

I didn't have time to answer as two vampires fluttered in blocking our way out. Alejandro threw himself into them, yelling for me to run. Pushing my body up the wall, I stood but I couldn't leave him alone to fight my battle, so I joined the fight, kicking the nearest body. The vampire turned his attention toward me, slamming me into the wall repeatedly until the pain became too much to bear, and darkness engulfed me.

A lovely but faint melody beckoned, luring me with its call. Little by little my senses awoke, such a strange sound – no instrument I had ever heard before. My body lay in clouds of soft, inviting comfort. My ingrained training kept my breathing steady as I tried to determine if I was alone, prisoner or safe among friends. Friends...my entire life I could count my friends on one hand. My father, Mace, Axe, Ji and...Val. I choked back the memory of my childhood friend, forcing the painful memories from my mind. All but Ji were gone, taken from this world by cruel hands. No, it was better not to care for anyone.

I froze at the touch of a tender hand wiping the tears from my face. "I know the pain is hard to bear," a sweet voice whispered. My eyes opened at the sound, further exposing the pain the memories I normally kept buried were wreaking on my mind. Staring down at me was a lovely version of Luken, the same clever eyes and cheekbones – a relative for certain. Moving to brush the wet from my face and regain my false bravado caused a painful chain reaction starting from my core and resonating through my skull. Gently she pushed my aching body back into the softness of the bed. "Luken said you are headstrong," she said as she raised a brow at me. "But you will do as I say or I will knock you out with a draught."

"You must be related to Luken," I replied, irritated that I didn't have the strength to resist her gentle push. "I recognize the sarcasm."

Her laugh was soft and traveled to her eyes. "Yes, he is my brother," she confirmed. Smiling down at me, she added, "I can see why he likes you. You are quite brave, especially for a woman." I tried to sit up once more, sucking in a sharp breath as pain ricocheted through my body. She let out a sigh as she reached for a bottle near my head and said, "Perhaps he exaggerated the depth of your wisdom."

I shook my head, instantly regretting the movement as the room started to spin. "I'll lie down, please don't drug me," I murmured. Completely embarrassed by my inability to suppress my emotions, I pushed my body deeper into the softness beneath me. Struggling for something to take my mind off the past, I asked, "What's your name?"

"Usoa, and you need not worry," she whispered as she turned her eyes back to mine. "I am no stranger to pain. I have seen bigger men than you succumb to tears. I will not tell anyone if the pain brings them, but there is no shame in it."

Relief washed over me with the realization she misunderstood my tears. "You speak English well," I said as she handed me a bowl of broth.

"Better than my brother, you mean," she giggled. Her smile faded with her next words. "My husband taught me as his charge requires him to speak several languages." Her eyes grew sad. "He practiced with me," she explained as she diverted her eyes.

With her obvious discomfort, I changed the subject. "Would you mind turning up the music?"

Her smile returned full force, but her eyes filled with mischief. "Certainly," she said as she gathered up her skirt. Turning, she revealed she had been kneeling at my bedside. I watched as she moved toward the foot of the bed, only then realizing we were in one of the wagons I had seen in the Roma camp. She swung the door wide and the music stopped. "The lady would like you to turn up the music," Usoa called out the door.

Luken's head popped up wearing a grin. "Back amongst the living?" he teased.

My spicy comeback was cut short as Alejandro shoved Luken to the side and locked his eyes on mine. "Beau," he whispered. Without taking his eyes from mine Alejandro extended a hand to Usoa to help her down before he fluttered to my side. From my peripheral vision I saw Luken smile as he shut the door. A strong calloused finger stroked my brow as Alejandro whispered, "Please tell me you are well, I have been so worried."

"I woke up with Usoa at my side tending my wounds," I said with a smile, "and I will be fine."

He closed his eyes and drew my fingers to his lips as he whispered, "I will not waste time trying to explain how foolish your actions were, but I will beg you to never do that again." His blue eyes fixated on mine. "Please promise me. I would be driven to madness if they killed you."

His eyes pleaded with me but he knew as well as I that no such promise would be made. Instead I pulled him close, drawing the sweetness of his tenderness in with each brush of our lips. Gently he crawled over me, nestling beside me and drawing as close to my body as he could manage without jostling me.

A tap came to the door. "Enter," Alejandro called out.

Usoa's eyes made brief contact with mine then shyly darted to the ground. "My apologies, I will return later."

"Don't be silly," I whispered. "This is your home. If anyone doesn't belong it is I."

Her eyes refused to make contact as she whispered, "What do you wish me to do, My Lord?"

Alejandro inquired, "Is she well enough I can care for her at my home? I have never liked the idea of you out here alone, but the thought of Beau here unprotected is unbearable."

"I would prefer to keep her close, but I believe the worst is behind us," she said confidently.

Thinking the answer was simple, I asked, "Would you consider joining us at Alejandro's home?" Alejandro's brows came together in frustration and Usoa shifted her weight back and forth at the suggestion. Confused, I said, "It seems the obvious solution, but I didn't mean to overstep by offering up your home, Alejandro."

Alejandro put on a charming smile then replied, "Of course Usoa is welcome in my home." He paused, struggling over a response, while Usoa's face ran an emotional gambit.

"Usoa cannot attend you in Alejandro's home!" Luken said matter-of-factly as he stepped from behind the door.

I watched Usoa's jaw clench as she set her shoulders defiantly, and said, "I will break camp and be there by nightfall." Turning, she glared at her wide-eyed brother, then added, "Do not presume to change my mind."

Luken stared at his sister's fleeing back then turned an ashen face on Alejandro. He shook his head as he whispered, "I care for Beau as well, but you know what this will mean. Please find another solution." Not waiting for a response, Luken turned to follow his sister.

"Why do I always feel like I'm missing something?" I asked.

Alejandro smiled down at me, and whispered, "It will take time to understand their ways."

I inquired further, "Did I say something wrong?" I let out a painful hiss as I tried to shift my position. "And don't you dare answer my question with a simple 'Their ways are not your ways.'"

He frowned at my discomfort but thankfully answered truthfully. "My home is considered unclean by her clan. No woman can enter without permission from the elders and a cleansing ceremony directly following. Only Luken is permitted to enter on a regular basis." Propping up on an elbow, he continued, "Her husband is currently exiled and she has chosen to live apart from the clan so that she may see him occasionally. If she does this they will surely shun her with no chance to regain her status within the clan should her husband's exile end."

Catching myself before I shook my head in confusion, I interjected, "How does anyone live with so many crazy restrictions?"

"I will admit their ways can seem restrictive, but every belief has its foundational cornerstones," he said as his finger stroked my cheek. "I should try to talk her out of it, but I find myself conflicted. I cannot lie, I want her help." His hand dropped and sadness crept over his features. "Still, it is far too selfish a request."

Staring up at his blue eyes, I suggested, "Perhaps I should stay here a few days. I wouldn't want to be the cause of something that would change her life forever."

"Though it would be the wisest course of action, I cannot let you stay here unprotected another night," he said boldly. Brushing a stray curl from my face, he added, "I am afraid I lost my heart." His lips brushed mine gently and I felt my heart flutter. "If I lose you my mind will follow. No, tonight you will be under the safety of my roof, no matter the cost."

Lost in the moment I barely heard Luken return to the doorway. He cleared his throat to draw our attention. His eyes bore a deep sadness as he spoke, "She will not alter her course."

"I am sorry, Luken." I choked out my regret. "I shouldn't have made the suggestion. I didn't know what it would mean."

The corners of Luken's mouth lifted slightly but his pain was clear. "The blame is mine," he said, "she is my responsibility while her husband is away."

"All of this is at my feet," Alejandro countered.

"No," Luken quickly replied, "my sister reminded me. It was my idea to bring Beau here. It was I that involved her and it cannot be undone." He looked intently at Alejandro, and said, "Neither will be safe here, as much as it pains me to admit, this is the only choice before us."

A few minutes later we rolled out of camp, but not before Usoa joined me in the wagon, dangling the dreaded draught before me. I had snarled at her offer but the first large bump had quickly changed my mind, and I let her dose me to ease the coming pain the trip would surely bring. I closed my eyes and let sleep take me, knowing that Alejandro was there to watch over me.

The next few weeks or rehabilitation inched by. They were only made bearable by my growing friendship with Usoa and the realization that I had fallen in love with Alejandro. I had yet to reveal the truth of the depth of my feelings for him, nor had he confessed his own, but there could be no doubt that the joy I felt when he entered the room, or emptiness a room held without him in it, was love.

Tucked away here in his home, far away from my previous life, made it almost possible to believe we might have a chance. Could I really live a fairytale? My heart pounded at the possibility. My mind, however, reminded me life had a way of kicking me in the teeth whenever I dared to smile. Still, tonight I had made plans to test my theory.

Usoa swept into the room wearing a huge smile and carrying a basket containing the items I asked for to make our dinner special. "Are you excited?" she asked.

"I knew I made a mistake telling you," I sighed.

"How else would you have gotten candles for your dinner date?" she teased. Her lips twisted in disapproval at my choice of attire. "You should wear a dress. Do not scowl at me! You could use more feminine choices in your wardrobe."

I laughed. "Any man interested in me wouldn't choose the word feminine to describe me."

"Make no mistake, Beau," she said with a smile. "You can't hide the woman in you. You might be strong, independent and forward thinking, but you are definitely all woman." She put the basket down and began poking and prodding me.

"I'm fine." I huffed. Her glance was skeptical, so I added, "My ribs don't hurt at all." She poked harder, watching my face as I held in the pain she inflicted.

Her sly smile let me know she knew the truth. "You're not combat ready quite yet." She observed. "And the dizzy spells?"

"Rare," I admitted, "if I get up too fast."

Batting her eyes at me, she said, "Then I give you my approval for your date this evening." Spinning on her heel she made for the door, calling back over her shoulder, "With one stipulation."

I called after her disappearing footsteps, "What are you up to, Usoa?"

"Me?" she asked innocently as she returned. Extending her arms, she offered me an emerald gown. "I would like you to wear this and let me do your hair."

I ran my fingers over the thick velvet gown. "It's beautiful," I said as I played with the beading on the bodice. Shaking my head, I stammered, "I couldn't. I've never worn anything this beautiful before."

"You can and you will," she demanded.

Without further argument I let Usoa have her way and soon was staring back at a Beau I didn't recognize. I had worn gowns on assignment but this was different. This time the gown I wore was for someone I cared for, someone I wanted to find me attractive for who I was, not someone I needed to get close to get information from or to kill.

She smiled at me in the mirror while fussing with a loose curl, stating, "He won't be able to resist you."

Alejandro's reflection appeared in the mirror and I spun to greet him. "I was going to ask who you were referring to, but I am hoping it was me." Slowly he walked toward me with his hand extended. "Please tell me I will be the lucky one on your arm tonight," he said as he took my hand in his, bringing it to his lips for a kiss.

As she brushed past us, Usoa giggled. "I shall be back shortly with your dinner."

"Give me ten minutes to change into something fitting of your beauty," Alejandro said as bowed over my hand then darted from the room.

Spinning in the dress I could barely contain my schoolgirl glee. Staring into the mirror I couldn't believe this was happening to me, all the loss in my life was for once truly a memory eclipsed by the joy springing from my heart. I ran my fingers down the dress, enjoying the feel of the fine fabric, resisting the urge to pinch myself – if this was a dream I didn't want to wake. Closing my eyes I prayed inwardly, *"Please let this be real, let me keep these people."* I felt him far before I saw him, and called out, "I can feel you breathing, Luken."

He chuckled as he emerged from the shadows and said, "I must improve my skills, it seems." He crossed the room and held out his hands, exclaiming, "Breathtaking! It is no wonder he is captive to your charms."

Squeezing his hands I teased him back. "Are all you Basque men so charming?"

"We are... protective of our family," he replied with a wide smile. "You are becoming a sister to me, so naturally I want the best for you." His comment struck me harder than I thought and tears threatened to spill over and ruin my makeup. He dabbed the corner of my eye with his sleeve, showing his understanding but not uttering another word. He hugged me briefly then silently left the room.

I sat down and surveyed the makeshift dinner table Usoa and I had set up for the evening. All of this was so overwhelming, beautiful, but so out of the norm for my life. I have undergone so many changes this past year, but nothing had prepared me for this – for Alejandro.

Alejandro found me lost in my thoughts, pulled back my hair, and ran his lips up my neck. "You are positively delicious," he whispered behind my ear. "Hold your hair up, I have something that will go with my mother's dress."

I was frozen by his words. Blinking back my shock, my hands flew to the gown. "Alejandro, I am sorry. I had no idea this was your mother's dress."

"If she could see you in it, my mother would insist you have it for your own. It was made for you, I am sure," he said as he smiled down at me. "Your hair, please," he insisted. Lifting up my hair I felt him slip something around my neck and fasten it in place. He took my hand and led me to the mirror.

I gasped as my eyes found the large red stone with rivers of green spiraling throughout set in pure silver. "It's beautiful, I've never seen anything like it."

"It's a bloodstone, and it has now found a home," he said with a tilt of his head.

I stared up at him in disbelief. "For me? Really?" He nodded with a smile. I pulled his mouth to mine, kissing him deeply. When he finally released my lips, I whispered, "Thank you, I love it."

We barely noticed when Usoa brought us dinner and for the life of me I can't recall what we ate. All I saw was the way he looked at me, all I felt was the fire he stirred within me, and all I could think about was the taste of his lips on mine. He must have been reading my mind because he dropped his napkin in his plate and pulled me into his arms. His kisses sent my head reeling – I couldn't get enough of him.

Lifting me in his arms he carried me to the bed, lowering me gently as his lips traced the lines of my neck. His erratic breathing drove me insane with the knowledge that he wanted me as badly as I wanted him. I pulled his body into mine, regretting only that the gown was so thick I couldn't draw him closer. Our hunger grew and I stared up into his intense blue eyes, captivated as I watched the transformation before me. I whispered, "Why do your eyes change like that?"

Misunderstanding, he turned his head as he answered, "When in battle or impassioned all our senses heighten, this changes the way our eyes refract light."

I pulled his chin back to me, staring lovingly into his eyes as I whispered, "Don't hide from me, you never have to hide anything from me."

Alejandro drove his lips into mine, reigniting the passion my question had quelled. His hands found the buttons of my bodice, quickly undoing them then pulling my body up till he could claim my breast with his lips. A moan escaped me and he responded with a fervor, propelling me to heights I never dreamed I could reach.

"Beau," he whispered between breaths. "We must stop." Ignoring his ramblings, I drove my tongue into his mouth, clinging to his every move. He groaned in pleasure and fire poured through my veins, igniting my passion further and I slipped out of the imprisoning gown. "I cannot," Alejandro said as he gently pushed me away. His face pulled tight with pain. "You do not understand the struggle within me."

I pushed, unmoved by his old-world values refusing to allow his lips to leave mine. "I want you to make love to me," I said with a smile. Pulling at the buttons of his shirt, I ripped it off and ran my tongue over his beautiful core.

I felt his body shudder in response. "My desire for you is clear, but I could not live with myself if I were to hurt you, Beau. What you ask is too dangerous in your current condition."

He started to get up from the bed. I moved quickly, wrapping my legs around his waist and pulling his body back into my own. I ran my lips up his neck, smiling to myself as I felt his breath quicken. "Alejandro," I whispered, "please." I let my lips nibble and explore the small space behind his ear and said, "I feel much better."

"You ask too much of me." A soft growl escaped him. The fever of his passion broke over the dam of his reserve, pouring over me as his lips sought mine. My body reacted to his touch as he pushed me down to the bed. "Your scent is overwhelming." He took a deep breath. I opened my eyes, watching every muscle in his face flex as he fought a silent battle within himself. His eyes caught mine; desire was almost tangible between us. I stared as his eyes turned to blue ice, piercing my soul as they held me captive. "If I lose control, run and lock yourself in the next room."

I arched my back closing the distance between our bodies, drawing his mouth to mine again. "You won't," I said as I brushed my lips against his. "I trust you."

He pulled away slightly, and asked, "How can you when I do not trust myself?"

"I trust you completely," I said as I slid my hands into the waist of his pants, pushing them down his legs.

His smile revealed the budding of his eyeteeth, the sight of them drew a strange hunger from me, and I launched myself at him. He forced me down into the soft sheets and buried his face in my chest, nibbling and sucking at my skin - calling forth tiny waves of pleasure. I moaned in delightful surprise as his fingers darted between my legs.

He groaned. "You have no idea the effect your scent has on me." He ran his tongue down my sides to the small of my stomach. "I want you, Beau," he whispered on my skin.

I confirmed, "You have me."

I ran my hands through his hair, pushing his head lower till his mouth claimed his prize. Lightning streaked through my body as he reveled in his mastery over my flesh, the resounding swells of bliss driving me wild. Fingers dug at the flesh of my hips, driving me deeper into his mouth till I could take no more. I tugged at his hands, my breathing erratic as I begged, "I want you inside me."

Seizing both my hands he shoved them above my head, sliding his free hand to my hip. His eyes blazed their passion into my soul, holding me prisoner despite the growing pain in my left shoulder. They maintained their hold on me as he thrust into my throbbing flesh. Despite my best efforts, my eyes fluttered at his strength.

He cried out in pleasure as he penetrated my womanhood. Each thrust probed deeper within me spreading a mixture of pain and pleasure unlike anything I had ever known. Our passion fractured my sense of reality till my mind and body could withstand no more. I arched up as my body released in sweet surrender. The action drove him wild, driving his fingers deeper into my flesh as his urgency demanded my body's compliance. His hips thrust forward with purpose as I felt his body tense for release, with his final thrust I felt a pop in my left shoulder and heard a scream escape my lips.

He smiled at me, drunk in the satisfaction of our union while my body writhed in agony beneath him, my shoulder dislocated by the strength of his passion. Realizing I was in pain he scrambled off me, inspecting the damage he had inflicted. His body rocked back and forth, tortured with the knowledge that his fears had manifested.

I tried to console him by saying, "It's just dislocated." A hand raked over his face, proving I chose the wrong words, so I continued, "I have had far worse." I forced a smile to my lips and said, "Just pop it back in for me and it's all good." Reluctantly his fingers gently probed my shoulder socket till he gave a half-hearted nod and forced my joint back into place. My scream echoed through the room. Instantly I regretted not being able to contain my pain.

Slowly he stood, his face devoid of all color as his eyes drifted over my body. When his eyes met mine they shot to the floor in shame. As he reached for his pants I caught his hand with my good hand, insisting, "Alejandro, I am fine."

He winced at my touch, murmuring, "Do not excuse my behavior."

Awkwardly I pulled myself up to his waist, clinging to him, afraid he was leaving the room when we should be celebrating our union. My words were muffled on his skin. "That was amazing. I have never experienced pleasure like that before."

Gently he pushed me away. "I pray you have never held such a selfish lover," he said under his breath.

My head snapped up in anger as I yelled, "Don't cheapen what we just had with guilt." I shook my head at him in confusion, asking, "How can you not feel the same? Even now I can feel your touch lingering on my body."

His eyes raked over me. "And tomorrow you will feel it fully," he said bitterly. "The welts from my touch are already painting your body. Soon the bruises will fully etch my sins upon your flesh." He removed my arm from his waist with care and moved out of my reach. "Leave me now, Beau, before I do something that cannot be undone - before I scar you for life."

My back straightened in defiance, and declared, "I won't leave."

His shoulders slumped as if I had hit him. As he walked toward the door, he murmured, "Then I will leave for both our sakes."

"You won't leave me," I yelled. "I know you want me. I know I'm right, this has to be right."

He paused at the doorway. "If I loved you, I would have never touched you," he called over his shoulder. "I would have fought harder to contain my lust. No, what I have done cannot be treated, unlike your shoulder. Go. Go back to your world, fall in love with a man deserving of your affection and leave this world behind you, Beau. You don't belong here." I wanted to run after him and beat the truth into him, but I was paralyzed by the fear of losing yet another person I had dared to love. My heart sank as his steps grew fainter, marking the growing distance between us.

CHAPTER ●——————EIGHT

The first few days I was sure he would walk through the door any moment. Those days rolled into weeks and still Alejandro had not returned. I didn't doubt he loved me, I knew it with everything within me, but I began to waiver on my belief he would come back. The belief took seed in my heart growing into a deep ache of absence of him. Why? Why did something so joyous have the ability to inflict such pain, rendering you paralyzed – love truly is a weapon, a double-edged sword of truth that I had no skill in wielding. How much loss could a person endure before they broke? How could I have let this happen? All the painful loss of my life visited me, vision after vision of those taken from me always circling back to Alejandro's blue eyes. Incapable of action or logical thought I lay in his bed, only Usoa's infuriating demands that I eat marking the passage of time.

Immersed in my sorrow I grew to hate the sound of her approaching footsteps, I considered killing her for her betrayal. Why could she not let this numbness drag me into the abyss of death? Each time she brought the tray I entertained dark thoughts of ending her life and ending my torture, but the tenderness in her eyes jolted me back to sanity and the hope he might return. The truth was I had grown to love her. It would only a matter of time before she was gone as well. It was my heart that had betrayed me, first by allowing Alejandro access, then Luken, and now his loving sister, Usoa. What was I becoming? Lost, completely lost... a pathetic fool.

Icy daggers of pain seared into my flesh, shocking me into the present. My eyes flew wide, finding Usoa standing over me preparing to dump another icy bucket of water upon me. Scrambling out from beneath her coming assault, I shouted, "What the hell do you think you're doing?" Despite my quick reflexes, she redirected the water halfway through the pour, further drenching me in the painful cold.

"I'm simply cleaning," she said matter-of-factly as the bucket clattered to the floor. Her eyes met mine defiantly. "You stink!"

Narrowing my eyes upon her, I whispered, "Do you realize how easy it would be to kill you?"

"Then do it," she yelled, throwing her hands into the air. "Anything would be better than watching you waste away in self-pity." The revolting revelation of her words hit me full-force, and her knowing eyes softened. "If he loves you, he will return," she said, placing a hand on her hip as a brow shot upward. "But you will not rot away any longer."

I let her push me down the hall to a waiting bath,

her voice echoing in my mind. She was right; living this way profited me nothing. As she poured the warm water over my head I let her wash away my weakness. I would not allow this newfound pain to rob me – I would take back who I am. I grabbed her hand as she reached for the shampoo, choking out, "Thank you." When she hesitated I smiled up at her and repeated, "Thank you." She smiled back her understanding and left the room, leaving me alone to scrub away the rest of my weakness.

It took a few additional days to develop a routine that hopefully over time would break the cycle I had allowed to take over my life. The first thing I did was ensure I was up and dressed before Usoa knocked at my door, refusing to allow myself the luxury of laying lifeless in bed. My ribs and shoulder had healed enough to allow for a daily workout and Alejandro had a room perfectly equipped to push my limits.

I ate meals with Usoa and listened as she worked through her own loss of the man she loved. Our time together brought a deeper understanding of her people and their relationship with Alejandro's family. She told me her husband was blood-sworn to Alejandro's brother, and as such was in forced exile from the clan. Her decision to stay at his side had inadvertently earned her a type of exile as well. Despite my inquiries, she never offered me information regarding Alejandro's brother, simply stated it was best not to speak of him nor of his crimes against the family. Her husband thought it was too dangerous for her to join him, but living apart from the clan made it possible for him to see her on those rare occasions he could steal away.

Usoa often watched when I worked the training dummies outside in Alejandro's courtyard, cheering when I did something she thought was spectacular. Every so often I was able to get her to engage a few strikes, but she refused to give up her skirts to truly learn. Her ever-roving clan was growing used to seeing me training outside, earning us fewer and fewer stares, but no one returned our smiles outside of Luken and Izar. Even Luken held himself afar, rarely speaking to us, but continuing to drop provisions mysteriously at our door whenever he was in camp. Asking him about Alejandro only earned me a sad shake of his head, and further silence.

On the rare nights Usoa would slip away to meet her husband, I explored the large house, hoping for some connection to Alejandro. Sometimes it felt as though he were there at my side, walking through the great rooms, explaining the history of this painting or that treasure. I knew I should be gracious and leave his home so he could return, but the thought made me sick and I was not ready for that finality.

It was on one of these occasions that I stumbled upon the entrance to the wine cellar. In the kitchen I leaned against a counter trying to decide what to nibble on when I felt the counter shift under my weight. Further inspection revealed a hidden passageway, one of many I had discovered during my explorations. Intrigued yet again, I followed the passage down a small set of stairs and discovered a treasure trove of fine wines. I recalled Alejandro telling me about his mother's side of the family making wine and how good the bottle was we shared on our first date.

Intent on choosing a bottle I ran my fingers over the many labels, wiping away the collected dust trying to find one written in English or bearing the same label I had shared with Alejandro at the inn. An intricately carved cabinet against the back wall drew my attention. Each door bore a rearing stallion, the same image that topped the blazoned shield hanging above the fireplace in the dining room. Alejandro had referred to it as his family crest as he explained the shield held the history of his family and their service to the church.

The doors groaned in protest as I opened them for what seemed like the first time in ages, if the thick layer of dust was any judgment of time. One half of the cabinet held bottles with a label bearing a flourished hand written letter E, while the other half was labeled with an A written by the same hand. Three bottles were missing from the side containing the E while the other still bore a full inventory.

There was no doubt within me that I had discovered a private label, and given each side of the cabinet held space for six bottles it seemed a limited reserve. My curiosity and intention to drink away my cares for the night drove me to select a bottle of each. I stared down at the undoubtedly rare bottles in each hand fighting with my conscience over my greed. With a sigh I gave into my selfishness as I admitted my sin out loud. "He shouldn't have left me alone. If he returns I will admit my larceny, and if not, he'll have to prove it was me."

After a quick stop in the kitchen for a glass and a bottle opener I started a hot bath, deciding a long soak would ease the soreness of today's workout. I tied my hair high on my head then turned my attention back to the two bottles, trying to decide which to uncork first. Deciding to start from the beginning of the alphabet I reached for the bottle with the A on the label. Popping the cork released a rich, fruity aroma filling me with anticipation as it mingled with the steamy air around me.

Armed with a full glass, I sank down into the

near scalding water, relishing the way the heat made my skin tingle. Unable to contain my urges a moment longer, I took a long pull of the deliciousness the glass held. Perfection ran down my throat, forcing my eyes shut with pleasure and making me reconsider wine as a favorite beverage. The corners of my mouth lifted as the thought that Alejandro should hurry home before I drained him of this particular treasure crossed my mind. Savoring my next drink, I let it linger in my mouth before my greedy stomach demanded I send it down.

Sinking deeper into the heat, I closed my eyes conjuring an image of Alejandro smiling down at me, his eyes turning lighter as his hunger for me grew. I let the fantasy draw me to his lips, trying to recall the fever that burned between us and sending up another prayer that he might return to me. A clash down the hall pushed the fantasy away as my eyes sprung open, seeking the source. "Who's there," I called out. "Usoa?"

Behind me, I heard the distinct sound of metal striking metal. Spinning around, I showered the floor with water in my haste, but found no one. I huffed out a breath as it occurred to me the sounds of the old house were playing tricks on my mind. Forcing myself to relax, I closed my eyes and took another long pull of beautiful red wine. Alejandro smiled down at me again, this time wearing that particular sideways grin he wore when something amused him. Another clatter in the hall bolted my body upright and sent my hand darting to the towel. Someone was humming, a woman, humming a sweet melody. It wasn't Usoa, but the voice was one I knew - oddly familiar. I couldn't place the tune, but somehow I knew I should know it by heart. Quickly I dried off and put on my favorite dress shirt of Alejandro's, careful not to slip on the wet floor.

My search of the main wing proved unfruitful. No one was there - even the courtyard was empty as the Roma had retired for the night. Returning to the bathroom I dipped a hand in the now cool water letting out a sigh of disappointment as I pulled the plug and watched the water drain from the tub. Reclaiming my glass and the two bottles I decided to climb into bed and waste the rest of the night in fantasies. As I neared the bed my head spun, assaulted by fleeting images, I reached for the bedpost for support. As I regained my balance I took another sip, only then realizing with a chuckle that I had not eaten dinner. It wouldn't be the first night I dank my dinner, but the wine was certainly making it to my head faster than normal.

After setting the bottles on the nightstand, I let my body drop to the bed wondering how many more nights would I waste waiting on a man who clearly didn't want me. How did this happen? Why? I ran my fingers through my hair and asked myself, "Who are you, and what have you done with my father's daughter?"

A giggle sent my body upright. My eyes blinked back surprise at the sight of my father's daughter sitting on the end of the bed, her bright blue eyes smiling back at me. The only problem... I'm an only child. I shook my head, trying to clear it and whispered, "Pull yourself together, Beau." *When I reopened my eyes she was still there, smiling, and there was no doubt in my mind that she was indeed my beloved sister. I found myself reaching for her dark braid out of habit, playfully tugging at it till she laughed. My heart melted with the sound. No, this was my little sister, of that I had no doubt. My eyes moved to her shoulder where my hand now rested, a man's hand.* My head shook in confusion. Reflexively I reached for another drink of wine. As the sweetness coursed down my throat my vision cleared and my sister faded from sight. I drained my glass and poured another, emptying the bottle of its contents. "I've lost my mind," I muttered under my breath then took another long pull of the treasure.

"Hello," a familiar voice called to me. I lifted my head, searching for the woman who owned the sound. I was suddenly kneeling at the feet of my

mother, a tall slender dark-haired beauty. She reached for my face, her fingers gently brushing my jawline as she spoke. "I am Ximenia," she said with a smile, "Alejandro's, and soon, your mother."

Shocked I could only stare up at this woman, a woman I knew so well but until this day had never laid eyes upon. I found her words amusing and could barely contain my mirth, something that greatly irritated her. "Alejandro, stop that! This is serious, you must focus," she stated with a raised brow.

"Yes Mother," I heard myself say.

She took my chin in her hand and her smile returned as she continued, "By now, you have come to know the secrets our family must bear." She paused, seemingly searching for her next words. "Now that you have taken the bridal wine and accepted his invitation to join with our family, your bonding has begun." She turned slightly and her voice lowered as she went on, "The coming events will be," again she hesitated choosing her words with care, "unsettling and change you, forever." She smiled down at me from over her shoulder. "Your event shall be different *than the one I endured, that shall be both my promise and my gift to you, for you will have me to guide you while I had no one at my side."*

From my right a loud, fat man laughed, drawing my attention. I turned my head and focus to him, as the room around me shifted to reveal a stable smelling of green leafy alfalfa and the robust aroma of a horse right after a hard ride. I swatted the flank of the giant black beast as I called out to the man, "Rub him down well, he fought valiantly today." As the man stepped forward to claim the reins of my favorite stallion, I shook my head, finally understanding what was happening to me.

The wine - I stared at the glass in my hand, it must contain Alejandro's blood. His memories! Closing my eyes once again I allowed the flood of his memories to whirl unhindered in my mind, less afraid of what was happening to me with the realization. My mind raced down fleeting moments in time. I clung to the intimacy of the time in the mind of the man I loved, cherishing what might be the last moments I ever have with him.

"Heed your right." my father scorned me as his practice blade struck my right thigh. My brother's laughter reached my ears, but I did not seek him out among the crowd. Instead I narrowed my eyes upon my target, dodging a second swing and earning a smile from my father. His blade came down upon mine and the force reverberated his vitality throughout my body and I was proud, proud to be his son.

The memory brought tears to my eyes as I let the current of the river of his remembrances carry me through time. The heavy smell of sweat landed me amid a once-lush field trampled to mud that now caked my boots, making it difficult to maintain my footing as the men I faced surrounded me. Made confident by their numbers, they sneered, calling out insults in their obscure mountain dialect. I felt the weight of another at my back, but I had no need to fear. My brother shifted his weight and laughed as he whispered, "Do they not know death waits for them at our hand?"

"They will shortly," I answered, earning a hearty laugh from the brother I trusted with my very life. "Let us finish this, I grow hungry."

"As do I," he growled in an unsettling way. As the men surged forward and the sound of metal vibrated through the air the image faded from my mind and the room around me returned to the cold hard reality that I was Beau and not Alejandro. I slumped to the bed, clinging to the remnants of his memories. I begged my mind to call up tears to relieve the painful lump growing in the pit of my stomach, but no tears remained, only the numbness of his rejection embraced me.

Closing my eyes tight I tried to summon his memories, but the harder I tried, the further they fled from my grasp leaving mere disorienting flashes. I reached for another drink, but the glass I held was as empty as the room surrounding me. In a fit of anger I tore at the shirt I was wearing and threw it in the far corner, staring at it as though he might manifest before me in some outlandishly magical way. "Come back!" I screamed at his shirt, but it laid there, lifeless, much like I had the first weeks after his abandonment.

Sullen, I wrapped myself in the silk sheet, hugging my knees to my chest, slightly rocking my body back and forth. My head swam with the potency of Alejandro's blood-laced wine, overcome with the desire for more of his memories I reached for the second bottle, quickly uncorking it and pouring its contents into my waiting glass. It wouldn't be till later that I would come to understand the recklessness of my actions.

This wine was earthier and had a slightly bitter aftertaste. There was something different in the very way the warmth of it spread through me. Where the first bottle felt cheerful and carefree, this one filled me with a guarded insecurity verging on paranoia, yet oddly powerful. "Hmmm," I wondered out loud as I swirled the wine around the glass, strangely attracted to the unique aroma.

My desire for the flavor grew with each sip, as did my desire for additional memories of Alejandro. *Closing my eyes, I sought him out in my mind, till the room changed and I found him astride the black stallion from the stable, his chain mail gleaming in the ebbing light day. He smiled at me, and the knowledge of his love for me filled me with pride, followed by the shame of a hidden secret. A secret I kept buried, kept locked away even from myself. I must not allow these thoughts to be revealed, I reminded myself.* Suddenly the room shifted back to a plain old room, the memories forced from my mind. Determined to share in Alejandro's memories, I refilled the glass and let it slide down my throat in large gulps, no longer feeling the need to enjoy the taste, simply eager to obtain results.

"Hello," a familiar voice called to me. I lifted my head again, staring up at the woman who owned the sound. The room shifted fully and I again knelt at her feet, but her joy was obscured by the pain I saw living in her sad blue eyes. "I am Ximenia," she said attempting to find a smile.

I covered my mother's hand with my own, and whispered, "This may wait."

Her hand stroked my cheek, as a tear escaped she said, "No son, the lessons of recent weeks have shown us the arrogance we have waved in the face of time." A half smile touched her lips as she began again, but my thoughts shifted to my beloved sister, and I let my mother's words fall away with the memories of my sister's idolizing eyes staring up at me.

The stone of our home broke away to a moss covered rock, my sister perched at my side as we fished in our favorite stream. Her line grew tight and her eyes lit up with the excitement of her first bite.

Our laughter filled the wood as she struggled to bring in her catch and turned to victorious hoots as she proudly held up the four-inch trout. I reached for her braid, but unlike the playful tug before, I rubbed my fingers over the intertwining folds of her braid, her adoring blue eyes engulfing me.

Terror consumed me as I was jolted in time to relive those same beautiful eyes screaming down at me as she stood helpless upon the eparchia wall. Dumbstruck, I felt my very heart explode with the realization no matter how hard I drove my mount; I would not make the wall in time to provide aid. My body writhed in pain as I watched her drug from my sight, swallowed by the distinctive sounds of flesh ripping and the trumpeting of death. Creepers!

Flailing against the mere hint of the carnage I discovered as I rode through the gate knocked my hand into the remaining bottle of wine. As I watched the red wine spilling out upon the floor, the memory of the blood-stained courtyard I rode into was too painful, drove me to the bleak, yet peaceful darkness of unconsciousness.

I opened my eyes slowly, regretting the action as the sunlight from the window dug into my hangover. He was standing at my bedside, staring down at me, the hunger in his eyes a bit more sinister than I recalled. He smiled when he saw I was awake. "Alejandro?"

His smile grew larger but his eyes seemed to be laughing as he responded, "Yes it is I, Alejandro."

His voice was off, rougher - not his usual clear baritone. Maybe I was dreaming, still asleep from drinking too much wine, or perhaps this was yet another memory aftershock. I tried to push through the cobwebs that the alcohol had left in my mind. "You came back for me," I said hopefully. My head pounded against distant memories of the prior night. I took a chance, reaching out my hand to prove he was real and invite him once again to my bed, hoping he would not reject me this time.

He reached down and pulled the sheet from my body, leaving me fully exposed in the morning air. His eyes took in every inch of me as hungry as the first time he had seen me. As his hunger grew I watched his eyes first deepen in color then grow lighter and lighter. I knew that look, he wanted me. "You beckoned." He teased. "How could I resist such a call?"

More games. I dropped my hand at his rejection. "I am not interested in your games," I said, not bothering to hide my irritation. "Run back to where you were hiding."

"I think not," he declared as he removed his shirt, revealing two descending scars on his chest.

Confusion clouded in my head. "You were hurt," I said as I closed the distance between us to inspect his new injury. I ran my fingers over the scars. "What happened? Why has this not healed like the ones before?"

"Your concern for my well-being, while unfounded is touching," he said firmly as he pushed me down to my back. I watched him as he freed himself from his remaining clothes. "By virtue of that tenderness I shall repay you in kind and be as gentle as my nature can allow." He traced my tattoo with his fingertips, starting at my toes. "This is quite lovely," he said softly. My heart raced as his cool fingers met my skin. He hovered above me, his eyes fully changed to ice blue with my body's reaction to his touch, running his fingers over my stomach as he continued his exploration of my tattoo. His voice grew deeper as he whispered, "Interesting that you chose a depiction of The Tree of Life." His fingers caressed my torso just under the swell of my breast. "Yes, I will try to be gentle." He turned me to my stomach, following the branches as they reached across my back and shoulder. His body pressed down upon me as he ran his fingers up and into my hair, pulling till my neck arched back and I could see his face. His mouth was inches from mine. "Declare you crave my attentions," he demanded, "and I shall make you my queen."

I whispered, "Alejandro, I love you." My lips

sought his as I tried to turn into his embrace but he held me firmly in place. He thrust himself into me, driving my breath from my chest. My anticipation of him outweighed the pain of his strength. His urges grew wilder with each lust-filled thrust. Something wasn't right. I struggled to get up, to turn so I could see his face, but he pushed me down deeper into the bed. "Let me up," I demanded.

He growled. "I am nearly ripe, hold yourself steady."

"I don't care what you are," I shouted as I rolled onto my back, twisting my body till I could shove my foot into his chest and launch him off my body. "What's the matter with you?" I demanded as I instinctively I covered my body with the remaining sheet and raced away from his reach.

"Now who's playing games?" He scoffed as he stalked me, his eyes examining my every move. "You're quite strong for a woman, worthy to be my queen, indeed."

Bewildered, I asked, "Alejandro, what is wrong with you?"

A fierce growl ripped through the air from my left. "Eneko! What have you done?" Alejandro stood in the doorway, his eyes stone cold. "You inglorious swine." He hissed. "You dare to claim what has been awarded me?"

There were two of them. My mind raced for answers. Twins. Disgust spread over me as quickly as the understanding that I had just been with his twin.

"Brother," Eneko acknowledged with a broad smile. "Welcome home, even if your timing is bad, as we were in the midst of a rather important event. I do not suppose you would grant a favor to return at a later time? My bride-to-be desires my company." He inclined his head in my direction, further taunting Alejandro's fury, then shrugged when Alejandro didn't bite and reached for his pants.

Alejandro's jaw clenched but he didn't look at me. "You are not welcome in this house," he informed his brother. "How do you find yourself here?" His body trembled with his growing anger.

Eneko spread his arms wide after pulling up his pants, and said, "Why, I have come to collect my bride, of course." His eyes dropped to the two empty wine bottles at the bedside. "Her summons allowed my entry."

Alejandro had slowly been making his way to stand between me and his brother. When he moved his hand at his side I threw myself forward to take hold of it. "She was not aware of what her actions would entail," he insisted.

Eneko tilted his head sideways, scoffing. "Nonetheless, I have claimed her, as is my birthright." He reached his hand forward, ordering, "Release her to me."

"Never." Alejandro growled. "Beau is not yours, nor will she ever be." He moved us to the corner where I had thrown his shirt the night before. I didn't hesitate to cover up. He shook his head as he inquired, "Don't you have two wives already? Or is it three now?"

A hearty laugh rolled from Eneko's lips as he queried, "My consorts?" He raised an eyebrow as he taunted, "They will understand that she is my queen and will learn their role. If my queen cannot tolerate them then they will be put aside. As long as Beau can satisfy my appetite, I shall no longer need their…" he paused then added, "attentions."

Alejandro tilted his head at his brother, a crooked smile crossing his lips as he changed tactics and said, "I would not expect a warm welcome when you get home. Especially from…" he paused searching his mind, "Iliana?" He pulled me back to his side but kept his eyes on his twin. "I see you did not discuss your intentions with her. She seems…" He mocked with satisfaction. "Rather upset."

Eneko spread his arms wide yet again, saying, "Do not concern yourself with my house, Brother."

With a snarl he added, "You made your choice long ago to walk away from my love for you." A wicked smile crept across his features as he demanded, "Now release my bride, I claim her as is my right. She has taken my blood, I received her offer and covered her first; our bond cannot be broken."

Anger flashed in Alejandro's eyes as he poured his anger out in a bark, "A full bond was not formed or I would be aware! I do not recognize your claim as it was taken in my name. Therefore, she belongs to me."

Eneko stretched his hand toward me, beckoning. "Beau, embrace me." I felt a tug within me, compelling me forward and watched a victorious grin spread across Eneko's face. "See, Brother? My blood lingers in her and her body desires my touch," he proclaimed proudly. "You are too honorable to risk making her into what you hate, but I can ensure the transition. With your lack of knowledge it's not possible for you to love her eternally, as I could."

"You are lying," Alejandro snarled. "You just hope to torture me with the possibility. We both know there has not been another Bloodknight since our sister was born." Disgust poured from his lips as he revealed, "Your demons slaughtered our entire *eparchia* - every last priest that could have held the secret." He laughed bitterly. "Do you expect me to forgive your sins, Brother?"

Eneko twisted his lips in pain as he answered, "I am painfully aware of my sins, there is no need for you to remind me of their horror. I know my soul is bound for hell." He replaced the sadness that spread across his face with a fake smile. "But it won't be today." His eyes narrowed upon his brother as he proclaimed, "And you are wrong, I *can* make her one of us. I shall make her my equal." He lowered his eyes looking at me through his lashes, his words somehow reaching into my soul. "Come to me, Beau, become my queen and rule at my side."

My feet inched toward him. I fought to resist his lure and willed them to stop. "I am not going anywhere with you," I stammered out. Then once the words found their way out, I took a step back and glared at him, reclaiming my self-worth.

Eneko smiled at me with new appreciation, and said, "Strong willed as well." He laughed loudly. "Alejandro, spare us the coming battle. I want her, and it is clear you do not, or I would not have been invited to her bed."

I felt Alejandro's body stiffen at the retort. Anger roared within me, and I shouted, "I am not a toy!"

Eneko raised his eyebrows at me, pursing his lips together, mocking my anger with widened eyes, asking, "Did I strike a nerve?"

I took a step toward him, and promised, "I'll wipe that smirk off your face."

"Do not let him goad you further," Alejandro stated as he caught my elbow. He let out a sigh and admitted, "I knew you would feel my tie to her." He drew me closer to his side. "I will not allow you to leave with her, neither will I allow your addiction to doom her to hell, even if I have to kill you."

"So you do love her?" Eneko asked, his brows coming together in a display of confusion. "How did you keep your feelings from me?" Eneko stared at me, then goaded, "Have you known him?"

"That is none of your business." I hissed.

"You have!" Eneko exclaimed. He shook his head in amazement, inquiring, "How did you hide her from me, Brother?"

Attempting to force the irritation from his voice, Alejandro said, "I am not playing games with you, Ene, we are no longer children. I will not allow you to make Beau some prize to be won, be content with the women you have chosen and leave mine alone."

Eneko squinted at his brother then asked, "Or?"

"You will join our sister and father in eternity," Alejandro promised. He pulled my hand to his chest, tilting his head down as he said, "Inform my brother that he is no longer welcome in your presence, and you do not desire his advances in the future."

"Beau," Eneko called softly, "I can lay pleasures at your feet that in your current state you cannot fathom." Something pulled at my chest as he continued. "I am the one you want, Beau; I will make you forget my brother exists." Pulses of pleasure danced on my skin as he stared intently into my eyes. Desire flared within me, I felt him pulling me to his side with unseen hands, his unspoken breath whispering his need to be in my arms. My lungs labored for air against his charms. He gloated. "You see how she responds to me after just a few minutes in my arms?"

Alejandro barked out my name. "Beau!"

Mustering all my strength, I shook my head clear, and whispered, "Eneko, I would like you to leave and not come back."

Eneko's smile faded with his defeat. "This is not over, Brother," he proclaimed. "Your bond is but a thread, far from established." He smirked. "After how many months with her at your side?" He bowed deeply to me and said, "Dream of me till next we meet, my queen." As the security of the unintended invitation receded, Eneko's discomfort grew. But, he stubbornly remained until he could endure the pain no longer. With a growl, he grabbed his shirt and quickly left the room, a trail of steam covering his retreat. Alejandro followed him, dragging me behind as he shadowed Eneko's fleeing steps until he was certain his twin had left the building.

After I was sure Eneko wasn't coming back, I gave into the weakness in my knees, slumping to the floor in shame. Despite my best efforts, tears broke through my defenses, further evidence of my betrayal. I choked back my regret. "What have I done?" Alejandro closed the distance between us, and I turned my face from his in shame as I barely whispered, "I will leave tonight."

"No," he said firmly, "I cannot protect you if you do not stay at my side."

I shook my head in disgust, insisting, "And I cannot stay knowing what I have done."

Alejandro knelt next to me, placing his fingertips under my chin, gently forcing me to look at him. "Beau, this is my fault not yours. I left you unprotected." His eyes closed and his voice grew softer as he admitted, "I was a fool to think I could hide you from him."

"You did hide me." My voice cracked as I uttered, "It was my mistake that brought him here. We both heard what he said."

He brushed the tears from my eyes as he informed me, "I also heard what he did not say. I know my twin, Beau, he was indeed aware of my..." He paused, pressing his lips together tightly.

"Just say it," I pleaded.

He shook his head as he muttered, "My feelings for you." He retreated from me, once again hiding behind his noble demeanor. "Your presence was not the complete surprise he would have us believe, he is planning something and it includes you. I was right to be afraid of his awareness of you."

"I love you," I confessed, disgusted that the first time I had said it out loud his brother had been the one to hear it. I ran my hands through his dark hair, demanding the truth, "Admit you love me. Tell me you can find a way to forgive me this betrayal, and I will stay." My eyes pleaded with him till I felt his walls crumble.

His voice softened as he reassured me, "Beau, there is nothing to forgive. You took my blood." He shook his head. "With it, you bound yourself to me. I saw, I felt it all. I know you thought you were giving yourself to me, he knew it as well. Eneko is to blame here, you hold no fault." He growled. Pulling my half-naked body into his arms, his eyes flashed as he admitted, "I do love you. So much it frightens me. You jumble my thoughts. My love for you makes my choices less clear." I smiled at him as he brushed my wild hair out of my face. "That I love you does not change the fact my love is lethal."

"You won't hurt me, I know you won't," I

215

whispered as I drove my mouth into his. His breath quickened with his desire for me, and his grip tightened. I bared my neck to him. "You know the solution." I wrapped my legs around his waist, pulling his body tighter against me. I watched his eyes change to the palest of blue, his desire quickening his breath.

He growled, "No, I will not." He buried his face in my chest as he fought for control. Slowly his breathing grew steady. "I am 659 years old and in all that time I have never found love. I will not risk your death with my bite, nor could I bear to see you slave to the thirst of a changeling."

Resting my chin on the top of his head, as I asked, "Where does that leave us?"

He planted small kisses in a trail as he nibbled his way up my neck to my ear. He whispered, "I love you with all that I am, but this is an impasse for which I have no solution." Alejandro pressed his forehead to mine. "I can only hope," he said as he kissed the side of my mouth. "To ask..." He nibbled at the other side. "Beg you to..." His lips swept along my jaw line till his cool breath brushed the lobe of my ear as he barely whispered, "Stay.

ACKNOWLEDGEMENTS

A huge thank you to: my mom, Betty, for a lifetime of love and support of my dreams;

my sisters, Shelly and Sheila, for putting up with my characters that seem to show up at every dinner we spend together;

Gregg, for his ever-faithful care and support;

my alpha and beta readers, especially Mal for always being there for me, and helping me fine tune my vampire lore;

my editor, Kathie from Kat's Eye Editing, for helping transform this manuscript into the final draft;

my CreateSpace team, for their attention to detail and always lending me an ear for my concerns;

the talented, Saidge42 for her cover artistry bringing Beau to life, and Laura Gordon-Moyer for bringing it all together, and her incredible work on my promotional package;

Melinda W. Burt, for her consult work and much needed mentoring;

and finally, my readers, for their inspiring anticipation. I trust I haven't let you down. If you enjoyed this book, please take a few moments to write a review. Thank you!

OTHER PUBLISHED WORKS
BY A M KRUSE

Coming Storm:

Book One of The Immortal Guardian Trilogy

The Rogue's Ladylove

96264249R00124

Made in the USA
Columbia, SC
23 May 2018